Captain of the Ship

A Caroline Classic
Volume 1

by Kathleen Ernst

★ American Girl®

Published by American Girl Publishing
Copyright © 2014 American Girl

Questions or comments? Call 1-800-845-0005,
visit **americangirl.com**, or write to Customer Service,
American Girl, 8400 Fairway Place, Middleton, WI 53562.

Printed in China
14 15 16 17 18 19 20 LEO 10 9 8 7 6 5 4 3 2

Cover image by Michael Dwornik and Juliana Kolesova

Cataloging-in-Publication Data available from the Library of Congress

*For all the readers who love
history and stories as much as I do*

*For my parents,
who filled our home with books*

*For Barbara,
who traveled to historic sites with me,
and for Stephanie,
who went to work with me*

Beforever

Beforever is about making connections.
It's about exploring the past, finding your
place in the present, and thinking about the
possibilities your future can bring. And it's about
seeing the common thread that ties girls from
all times together. The inspiring characters you
will meet stand up for what they care about
most: Helping others. Protecting the earth.
Overcoming injustice. Through their courageous
stories, discover how staying true to your own
beliefs will help make your world better
today—and tomorrow.

TABLE *of* CONTENTS

A Fine Sloop

CHAPTER 1

June 1812

aroline Abbott leaned over the rail and laughed with delight. "Isn't this *wonderful?*" she asked her cousin Lydia. Sailing on Lake Ontario was fun any time, but being permitted to come aboard the sloop *White Gull* on its very first voyage was an extra-special treat.

"It's marvelous," Lydia agreed. "I'm glad that Oliver and your papa invited us."

Caroline's father had built *White Gull* for Oliver, Lydia's older brother. "You're lucky to get command of such a fine little sloop," Caroline told Oliver, who was steering the ship.

"*White Gull* still belongs to your father," Oliver reminded her. "It will take me some time to earn enough money to pay him back." His voice dropped. "I just hope America doesn't decide to go to war with Great Britain before I can do so," he muttered.

"Let's not talk about that today!" Lydia said impatiently.

Caroline felt impatient, too. She'd listened to adults arguing about whether America should declare war on Great Britain all her life. Caroline didn't want a war. She didn't even want to *think* about a war.

The breeze whipped some strands of hair into Oliver's face. He paused to retie his hair behind his neck. "It's been thirty years since America won its independence from Britain. Maybe President Madison can avoid fighting another war."

Caroline wanted to change the conversation from war to a happier topic. "Now that the sloop is finished, you can sail all around Lake Ontario!"

Oliver grinned. "I'm looking forward to buying and selling goods along the lakeshore. It's a fine way to earn a living."

"You can start by buying some embroidery silk for me!" Caroline said.

Oliver shook his head. "Mistress Abbott, I will gladly haul sailcloth and tar for your father, and apples and potatoes for farmers. I will happily carry mail, and take passengers wherever they wish to go. But surely you cannot expect me to shop for embroidery silk!"

Caroline smiled mischievously. "I need something of a reddish brown. Like cinnamon, but with more red."

Lydia giggled as Oliver made a face.

"And *then*, some lace," Caroline continued. "Mama is helping me make a new dress for my tenth birthday. A bit of new lace would be perfect."

"Enough teasing," Oliver begged. "I'm a merchant, not a lady's maid!"

"Why do you think I'm teasing?" Caroline asked. She held her head high, the way Lydia did when she was pretending to be a fancy lady. Lydia, who was almost twelve, giggled even harder.

"Oliver?" Papa called in his no-nonsense captain voice. "Watch that you stay on course. And you girls— remember to stay clear of the mainsail."

"We'll stay clear," Caroline promised. Really, Papa didn't need to remind her about every little thing! She'd been born on the shore of Lake Ontario, and she'd been sailing with him for as long as she could remember. Papa was the finest shipbuilder on all the Great Lakes. And one day . . .

"What are you thinking about?" Lydia asked. "You have a dreamy look on your face."

Caroline hesitated before bursting out with it. "One day, I'm going to ask Papa to build *me* a sloop. I'll be captain." It was her most precious wish, one she usually kept tucked away in her heart.

Beneath her bonnet, Lydia's eyes went wide with surprise. "You can't be captain of a ship!"

"I *shall* be," Caroline insisted. "After I finish learning to be a good sailor. Would you like to be on my crew? We'll sail all the way to China!"

"China?" Lydia squealed. Neither girl had traveled farther than back and forth across Lake Ontario.

"Yes, China," Caroline declared. "We'll visit the markets there and bring back gifts for our families."

Lydia shook her head. "I don't think I want to go to China," she said. "I want to get married and live in a fine house in Kingston and have six children. All girls."

"Well, then, I will have to bring back *lots* of gifts," Caroline said. "Dolls and fancy hair combs and pretty bowls for your daughters' oatmeal."

"And a silk shawl for me?" Lydia asked.

"Yes," Caroline promised. Then she turned to look

at Oliver. He stood at the back of the boat with feet braced. He leaned into the tiller, a long wooden bar used to steer the ship. The breeze ruffled his hair as he looked over the lake.

Caroline couldn't hold in a little sigh. There was no finer feeling than being aboard a sloop on a fair day. Sailing made Caroline feel as free as one of the gulls soaring overhead! She had tried not to envy Oliver while the men at Papa's shipyard built *White Gull*. It had been difficult, though. Sometimes envy sat in her chest like a cold, hard lump.

"Wind's shifting," Papa called.

"Yes, sir," Oliver said. He edged the tiller over a little farther. The sails made satisfying snapping sounds as the heavy cloth caught the breeze. Since the ship held no cargo today, it skimmed lightly over the waves.

"Caroline, what direction is the wind coming from?" Papa asked.

Caroline closed her eyes, trying to tune her senses to the day as Papa had taught her. She could smell the water, and the faint tang of newly dried paint, and the heavier scent of tar. She heard waves slapping the ship's hull, and the familiar rattle of the lines that controlled the sails, and the steady creaking of wooden timbers beneath her feet. And she felt the wind against her face.

She opened her eyes. "The wind's from the west, Papa!" she called.

He nodded. Caroline felt the lump of envy in her chest melt away. *I can make Papa proud of me*, she thought. If she kept learning all she could about sailing, perhaps one day he would build her a sloop of her very own.

"I feel as if we're flying," Lydia exclaimed. She leaned over the rail, watching the water rush by below. "We might as well be on a flying carpet!"

"*White Gull* is certainly colorful enough to be taken for one," Papa grumbled.

Caroline hid her smile. Papa liked to paint his ships a plain gray. After many discussions, though, Oliver had convinced Papa to paint this ship bright blue, red, and yellow. Oliver wanted his future customers to recognize his ship easily, even from far away.

Lydia straightened and tugged on the brim of her bonnet. "It is very bright today," she complained.

"I like it." Caroline tipped her head back so that she

could feel the June sunshine on her face. The winters in northern New York were long and cold. Caroline didn't see what harm it did to enjoy the sunshine while they had it.

"Young ladies must protect their skin from the sun," Lydia said.

Caroline sighed. Lydia sounded as prim as Mrs. Shaw, a neighbor who was fond of finding fault with Caroline. Lately, Lydia had started acting as if she wanted to be all grown up. Caroline wished Lydia would forget about fancy manners—at least for a little while.

She reached inside the small knitted bag she'd carried on board. "Look what I brought!" She pulled out a small top, made of wood and painted green.

"Can we play with it on board?" Lydia asked doubt- fully. The girls had spent many hours practicing with it at Caroline's house, perfecting their ability to make the top spin.

"We can try," Caroline said. "Let's go up near the bow. That's the front," she added, remembering that Lydia didn't know ships as well as she did. "And don't forget—always keep one hand on the rail for safety."

After making their way forward, the girls sat down a short distance apart. Caroline paused, feeling the deck tilt back and forth beneath her. She tried to time her spin, aiming the top so that it would travel down the slope to Lydia.

"Got it!" Lydia cried, snatching the top before it wobbled out of reach. "Now let me try."

With some practice, both girls were soon using the ship's movement to help send the top exactly where they wanted it to go. Caroline grinned when Lydia pushed her bonnet back to get a better view of the top spinning across the deck. Maybe Lydia wasn't *quite* ready to be all grown up after all.

Papa interrupted Caroline's thoughts. "Are you paying attention to the wind?" he called to Oliver. "You need to change the mainsail."

"Yes, sir," Oliver answered. "I'll do it."

Caroline paused. She knew that sailors had to be aware every minute of the way the changing wind affected the sails. They used the wind to keep the ship heading where they wanted to go. Papa had decided that *White Gull* needed to change course.

"No more play for now," she told Lydia. "Hang on,

and stay down!" The girls squeezed against the rail, well out of the way.

Papa stationed himself by the ropes that helped control the huge sail. Oliver began shouting commands that any sailor would understand: "Prepare to jibe! Trim the sheet!"

"He's trying to sound like your father," Lydia whispered.

And one day, Caroline thought, *I shall be the one giving those commands.*

Oliver pushed the tiller hard and let the mainsail begin its swing far out over the water. The sloop shuddered as the wind hit the loose sail. Caroline instinctively clenched the rail with both hands. The top slipped from her fingers. It skittered across the tilting deck.

"Oh!" Caroline gasped. As she reached to grab the toy, she felt the rail slip from the fingers of her other hand. Suddenly she too was skidding across the slanting deck.

"Caroline!" Papa bellowed. Oliver shouted a warning. Lydia screamed.

Caroline was tumbling too fast to answer. Her

hands burned as they scraped along the deck. She bounced against a wooden storage box, and pain stabbed through her shoulder.

I must stop! she thought frantically. If she got in Papa's way as he wrestled with the ropes, it could mean disaster for the ship. If she got tangled in the ropes, she could be seriously injured. And the heavy beam at the bottom of the sail, called the boom, was swinging across the deck with enough force to knock into the water anyone and anything in its way. Time seemed to slow as Caroline crashed and rolled across the deck. Finally she bumped against the far-side rail. She wrapped her arms around it and hung on with all her strength as the sail swung out over the waves.

It felt to Caroline as if the wind would yank the sail from the mast altogether—and maybe even overturn the ship! But Oliver had learned well. He knew just how long to wait, just the right moment to move the tiller again. After a lurch, the sloop settled politely on a better course.

Caroline struggled to her feet, keeping one hand clenched on the rail. She felt banged and scraped and bruised all over.

"Are you all right?" Lydia asked, hurrying to join her. Then Papa appeared, and Lydia stepped back. Papa's face looked like a thundercloud.

"I'm all right," Caroline said in a small voice. "And I'm sorry."

"What were you *thinking*?" Papa demanded. "You could have been knocked overboard—or even killed, if the sail had hit you! Haven't I taught you better?"

"Yes, sir," Caroline said miserably. "But—it was an accident! I dropped my top, and I was afraid it might fall into the lake, so I tried to grab it. And then . . ."

Papa glared at the toy, which had come to rest innocently nearby. He snatched it up and stuffed it into his pocket. "There is no room for such play on the deck of a ship!"

"Yes, sir," Caroline said again. Her lower lip trembled. "I just thought . . . that is, you and Oliver had everything set, and—"

"You must be alert every moment when you're on board a ship!" Papa interrupted. "It's not enough to set sail once. Winds shift constantly, and you must always be ready to adjust your course. Out here, everything can be lost in an instant."

"I understand," Caroline whispered.

Papa shook his head. "I don't believe you do. You're too flighty, Caroline. If you want to sail on the Great Lakes, you must stay *steady*. Watchful, every moment."

Caroline's skin grew hot. Papa turned and made his way back to Oliver.

Oliver gave him the tiller before joining the girls. "Don't feel sad," he told Caroline. His tone was kind. "No harm was done."

"I've disappointed Papa," Caroline said.

"No, you frightened him," Oliver said. "That's why he got angry."

"All that matters is that you didn't get hurt," Lydia added. "Gracious! Perhaps you should stop dreaming about a ship of your own."

I won't, Caroline thought stubbornly, although her heart felt as heavy as an anchor. She'd have to work extra hard now to prove herself to Papa.

Lydia tugged her bonnet forward again and gazed out over the water. They had almost crossed the lake. The roofs of Kingston, in Upper Canada, had come into clear view. "Why doesn't your father just put in for Kingston now? You and I could visit the shops."

"He says we don't have time," Caroline said. "We'll drop you off at the landing below your farm."

Oliver cocked his head, sniffing the air. "The wind's dying," he said.

With all the commotion, Caroline hadn't noticed the shift in the weather. The sails, with no wind to fill them, made flapping sounds. The deck motion had gentled. She darted a look at her father, half hopeful and half fearful. Sometimes, when the wind was no more than a soft breeze, he let her practice steering.

He caught her glance. After a moment, his stern expression softened. He beckoned with one hand. Caroline's heart rose. She hurried to join him at the tiller.

"Thank you, Papa," she said. She braced her feet, grasped the polished wooden tiller carefully, and leaned against it. Papa stepped close behind her, putting one strong, calloused hand on the tiller for guidance and the other on her shoulder. Caroline inhaled his familiar, pleasant scent of pipe tobacco and sunshine, mixed with faint traces of sawdust and turpentine from the shipyard.

"Ease her over a bit," Papa instructed. "That's it."

Caroline concentrated as hard as she could. She could feel the ship beneath her feet, responding to each adjustment.

All too soon, however, the little sloop was barely moving. "We're becalmed," Papa announced. "No trouble, though. The wind will come up again."

Caroline glanced toward Kingston. They'd drawn near enough that she could easily make out the town's wood and stone buildings. Several ships bobbed in Kingston's harbor. Upper Canada was a British colony, just as New York had been years ago, before the United States won its independence.

Papa stepped back, put both hands on Caroline's shoulders, and turned her to face him. "You made a mistake today, daughter."

"I know, and I'm *very* sorry." Her words seemed to tumble over each other in their eagerness. "I'll do better, Papa. I *promise*."

"Very well, then." Papa nodded.

"I can be a good sailor, Papa," Caroline said. She wanted so much to make him understand! "I know I can. Would you . . . do you think you might build a ship for me one day?"

"Now, Caroline." Papa brushed a stray curl back from her face with a gentle thumb. "I know you love sailing as much as I do, but you're just a child. And a girl as well."

"I mean when I'm older," Caroline explained. "I can be a good captain, even if I am a girl!"

Papa looked over the water. Finally he said, "I can't say yes or no today. I'd be a poor father indeed if I made a promise I wasn't sure I could keep! I didn't go into business with Oliver until he'd proved himself capable of it, and he's ten years older than you. Do you understand?"

Caroline looked at her shoes, trying to hide her disappointment. She didn't *want* to understand. She wanted Papa to have confidence in her, and to trust that one day she'd be ready.

Papa lowered himself to the deck. "Sit," he invited Caroline, patting the sun-warmed wood. Caroline settled down beside him, still struggling to bury her hurt feelings. Papa rummaged in his pocket and pulled two lengths of cord free. He handed one to Caroline. "Have I ever shown you how to make a Flemish knot? Here, watch how I do it."

Caroline leaned close, trying to follow along with her own cord as Papa wove the two ends of his cord together.

"No, over and under this way." Papa showed her again.

"I think I've got it," Caroline said after a moment. She tied another Flemish knot, this time on her own. "There!"

"Keep practicing," Papa told her, tapping the cord. "Sailors practice their knots so often that when they need to make one quickly, their hands remember how."

Caroline began another Flemish knot. By the time she'd made three in a row, Lydia and Oliver had joined them.

"Uncle John," Lydia asked, "will you tell us a story?"

Papa began filling the bowl of his pipe with tobacco from a little pouch. "Well, the first ship I built was a sloop not too different from this one. Try to imagine sailing twenty years ago. There weren't many towns around Lake Ontario then, so I worked on a big river east of here. After I met and married Caroline's mother, we worked together on the ship. Sometimes we just hauled freight. Other times we carried passengers. We'd anchor up at night, and there would be singing and even dancing under the stars."

"Oh," Caroline breathed. "That must have been lovely."

Papa smiled. "It was a fine life. Sloop captains would pull up alongside each other to exchange news. A few times, well after dark, I saw glowing torches along the river shore. Indians used the torches as they speared fish at night. And—"

"Uncle John!" Oliver called sharply.

Papa scrambled to his feet.

"Has the wind picked up?" Caroline asked, although she could tell it had not—not very much, anyway. Then she heard a splash. It came from the Kingston side of the ship. She followed the others to the rail.

Three longboats were coming straight toward *White Gull*. Even from this distance, Caroline could see the British flag hanging limply over the boat. The men pulling on the oars wore blue and white uniforms. Each boat held about twenty men.

"Why are they working so hard to reach us?" Caroline asked.

Papa crossed his arms over his chest, frowning. "Something's wrong," he muttered. "I don't like this at all."

Terrible News

aroline shoved the knotted line into her pocket with suddenly trembling fingers. "Papa?"

"You girls get below and stay there," he ordered.

Caroline and Lydia exchanged a wide-eyed look. Caroline's heart fluttered as she hurried down the steps to *White Gull*'s hold beneath the deck. There was a tiny galley for cooking, a couple of bunks, and empty shelves where Oliver would store barrels of flour and potatoes and whatever else he might haul.

Lydia followed her below. "What do you think is wrong?"

"I can't imagine!" Caroline said. For a few moments the girls waited in uneasy silence. Then Caroline turned back toward the steps.

"Caroline, stop!" Lydia hissed. "Your papa said—"

"I'm not going up on the deck," Caroline said in a low voice. She crept up the steps, crouching at the top so that she could listen.

"What's happening?" Lydia asked in a hoarse whisper.

"The British men are pulling closer," Caroline reported. "I can hear the little splashes from their oars."

A shout cut the afternoon: "*White Gull!* Strike your sails and prepare to be boarded!"

Caroline frowned. The British men were acting as if they owned all of Lake Ontario!

Papa's voice was forceful but calm. "What is your business with us?"

"Sir!" It was the same voice. "Prepare to be boarded at once, or we will open fire!"

Lydia gasped, and Caroline's mouth went dry. Open *fire*? Why would the British men threaten to shoot? Papa and Oliver hadn't done anything wrong!

She peeked around the corner just as the *Gull's* wood-and-rope ladder clattered against the ship's hull. A moment later, a tall hat popped above the rail. Then the man wearing that hat appeared, in a blue and white uniform coat with gold buttons. He swung one leg over the rail and jumped to the deck. Several sailors climbed on board after him.

"Explain yourself!" Papa demanded.

The British officer lifted his chin, looking haughty. "I am Lieutenant Morris. I—"

"We are an unarmed ship from Sackets Harbor," Oliver interrupted. "We're not carrying cargo."

Go away, Caroline ordered the British man silently. *Just go away!*

Papa planted his feet a little more firmly on the deck. "You have no right to threaten this vessel."

The British officer let one hand rest on the hilt of the long sword hanging by his side. "I have every right, sir," he snapped. "Perhaps you have not yet received the news."

"What news?" Papa's tone was hard. Caroline could tell that he was very angry.

The British officer gave him a small, cold smile. "Why, of war, sir."

War? Caroline's stomach clenched. She heard Lydia gasp.

Lieutenant Morris paced a few steps, studying the sloop. "Your American president has declared war on

Great Britain," he continued. "I am seizing this vessel in the name of His Majesty King George the Third. You are now my prisoners."

No! Caroline wanted to scream. *No, no, no!* But the words felt frozen inside.

"My father is a British citizen who lives in Upper Canada!" Oliver cried. "You have no cause to seize this ship."

"This ship is flying an American flag," said Lieutenant Morris. "My duty is clear."

Oliver launched himself forward with an angry snarl. Caroline's heart seemed to leap into her throat as the British sailors reached for their weapons.

Papa managed to grab Oliver. "Think of the girls," Papa muttered.

Oliver instantly went still.

"We have two young ladies aboard," Papa told Lieutenant Morris. "I trust that my daughter will be safely returned to her mother in Sackets Harbor. At *once*. And—"

"Papa, no!" Caroline cried. All the men's heads turned as she scrambled into the open.

"Caroline, be still," Papa said in a voice so stern

that she swallowed her protests.

Then Papa turned back to the British officer. "And my young niece lives not three miles from here. Will you make provisions for the girls?"

"Why—why, of course." Lieutenant Morris's voice had lost its mocking tone. "Your niece will be given safe haven in Kingston until her parents can fetch her. I will escort your daughter back to Sackets Harbor myself, under a flag of truce. I give you my word."

Papa left the knot of men and crouched in front of Caroline. "I know what's best, daughter," he said, taking her hands in his.

"I don't want to go with them," Caroline whispered.

"I know," he said gently. "But you must obey me, and be brave."

Caroline stared at Papa through tears. She didn't feel brave at all. Lydia had come on deck behind her, and she stood clinging to her brother. Lydia looked as if she wasn't feeling brave, either.

"Remember, you are a sailor's daughter," Papa told Caroline. "Everyone must sometimes face stormy seas. Good sailors learn to ride the storms through to better weather. Can you do that?"

"I—I'll try."

"Stay steady, Caroline. Obey your mama. Give her and your grandmother whatever help they need while I'm away." Papa's voice was urgent. "I must have your *promise*."

Caroline swiped at her eyes with one hand. "I promise, Papa."

"Make me proud." Papa squeezed her hands before rising. He looked at the lieutenant. "Let's get on with it."

As Lieutenant Morris snapped some orders to his men, Lydia gave Caroline a fierce hug. "Good-bye," she whispered in Caroline's ear.

"Good-bye," Caroline echoed. She felt numb inside. When would she see Lydia again? When would she see *any* of them again?

Lieutenant Morris pointed to the longboat still bobbing right beside *White Gull*. "If you please, child," he said to Caroline.

Caroline wanted to yell, *I am not your child!* But her voice seemed locked inside her throat again. The best she could do was ignore the helping hand he offered. She climbed down the ladder into the longboat. Her knuckles got scraped, and she had to kick her skirt aside as she planted her feet on the rungs. Once she was in the vessel, she sat with her knees pulled up close and shoulders hunched, staring at her lap.

Lieutenant Morris and some of his sailors came down the ladder and settled into the longboat. Caroline felt the boat lurch forward when the sailors began pulling on the heavy oars. As the longboat moved away from *White Gull,* she couldn't help looking over her shoulder. Papa sat straight as a mast in one of the other longboats. Lydia was climbing down the ladder to join him, and Oliver waited his turn. The British sailors dropped the *Gull's* sails.

Caroline felt an ache inside her chest. One tear spilled over and slid down her cheek. She swiped it fiercely and bent her head again. *I will not cry,* she told herself, over and over. *I will not let them see me cry.*

A Sad Homecoming
≥ CHAPTER 3 ≤

Soon the wind picked up, and the British men were able to raise a small sail in the longboat. Caroline kept her head lowered, refusing to look at the sailors who had taken her father prisoner and stolen *White Gull.* After what seemed like forever, she heard the rattle of rigging lines banging lightly against the masts of several anchored ships, and she knew they must be approaching Sackets Harbor. She was home.

She looked up. The little village of Sackets Harbor sat on the shore of a natural harbor, protected from Lake Ontario's sometimes-fierce wind and waves by a protective curl of land. A little log blockhouse perched on a rise. That was where American soldiers watched over the port and protected its ships. Caroline hoped that the Americans would come and arrest Lieutenant Morris!

As she watched, the Abbotts' house came into view up the hill from the harbor, on the eastern edge of the village. Caroline pictured Mama and Grandmother inside, polishing pewter or cleaning fish for supper, not knowing what terrible thing had happened.

"Show us where to land, child," Lieutenant Morris called. He pulled a large white handkerchief from his pocket and waved it above his head. Caroline knew that white handkerchiefs or flags were used to signal a truce. The lieutenant was telling the American soldiers not to shoot.

Caroline pointed toward the dock at Papa's shipyard. Just knowing that Papa's workers were nearby made her feel safer.

The longboat moved through the harbor. On the American navy ship *Oneida*, which was anchored there, sailors gathered at the rail to watch. Two Seneca Indian men canoeing past with baskets of whitefish to sell stopped paddling and stared. Caroline heard shouts from the landing. Several workmen lifted their heads and pointed.

Lieutenant Morris's sailors maneuvered the longboat beside a wooden ladder nailed to Papa's dock.

Caroline jerked up her skirt with one hand and half-stepped, half-tumbled over the side of the longboat. Her foot slipped from the rung she'd aimed for. Icy water clamped around her leg, knee-deep.

One of the British men held out his hand to her. "Here, now, let me help you," he said.

"I don't want your help!" Caroline yelled. She clenched the ladder and managed to find a foothold. Climbing up a ladder in a wet skirt was even harder than climbing down.

The dock trembled beneath heavy footsteps as Papa's chief carpenter ran to meet her. "What's this?" Mr. Tate demanded. "Miss Caroline?"

"I have delivered the young lady," Lieutenant Morris shouted, waving his handkerchief again as the longboat pulled away. "As I promised her father I would."

Caroline glared at the lieutenant. "We didn't even know that a war had started!" she shouted after him. "What you did is not *fair*!"

"War?" Mr. Tate stared at the departing longboat. "*War*, you say?"

"President Madison has declared war on Britain!"

she told him. "That British officer took Papa and Oliver prisoner, and seized *White Gull*!"

Mr. Tate sputtered, "Why, those—I could just . . ." His hands clenched into fists.

Caroline grabbed his arm. "I have to find Mama, but please—go tell the navy men. Before some other American ship gets captured."

He gave one grim nod and pounded down the dock. Caroline ran after him, shoes squishing, her clammy skirt clinging to her legs. She ran through the shipyard and past the warehouses, shops, and market stalls near the harbor. Turning up the hill, she dodged a man balancing a large toolbox on one shoulder and a woman selling candles from a tray. "Isn't that the Abbott girl?" someone asked. Caroline kept running.

Her lungs felt ready to burst by the time she'd run up Main Street's hill and turned left onto the lane that led to her own home. She passed the Shaw house, and finally—up ahead was her home. And there was Mama, cutting rhubarb in the garden.

"Mama!" Caroline croaked.

Mama glanced up, then scrambled to her feet and ran to meet her daughter. "Caroline? What is it?"

She grabbed Caroline's shoulders. "What's wrong?"

Caroline's words came out in breathless bursts. "The British . . . took Papa . . . prisoner! Oliver, too."

Mama turned pale. *"What?"*

"And they stole *White Gull.* They said we're at war!"

Mama clutched Caroline close in a tight embrace. "Heaven protect us."

Half an hour later, Grandmother put a cup of steaming ginger tea on the table in front of Caroline. "Drink up," she ordered. She was a white-haired woman with stooped shoulders who moved a little more slowly with every passing year. Her blue eyes could spark with impatience, though. Caroline picked up the cup and sipped.

Mama was striding back and forth, her heels clicking angrily against the floorboards. "How dare they!" she muttered again.

Grandmother sat down in her chair by the kitchen fireplace, where she could warm her bones. "There is nothing the British won't dare," she said quietly. Caroline knew that Grandmother was thinking about her husband, who had died fighting for America's independence during the Revolutionary War.

Mama stopped pacing and looked from Grandmother to Caroline. Her voice was as firm as an oak plank. "Thirty years ago, British soldiers killed my father," she said. "I will *not* allow British soldiers to imprison my husband and nephew now. Not without trying to win their freedom. Do you hear me?"

"Yes, ma'am," Caroline whispered. Still, she didn't see that she and Mama and Grandmother had any choice. Papa, Oliver, and *White Gull* were gone. And Caroline was desperately afraid that she would never see any of them again.

Caroline jumped when someone knocked on the back door a moment later. The young man who stepped inside was all long arms and long legs, and skinny as a fence rail.

"Seth, I'm so glad to see you," Caroline said. Seth Whittleslee was only a few years older than Caroline. He was the local post walker, tramping up and down the lakeshore delivering news and mail. Sometimes he even crossed the border into Upper Canada, so Caroline was never sure when she'd see her friend next. When he could spare a day, though, he and Caroline went fishing together.

"Is it true?" Seth demanded. "I just heard that the British seized *White Gull* and took your father and Oliver and Lydia prisoner!"

"They said Lydia could go home. But the rest is true." Caroline quickly told her friend what had happened.

"Well, I think it's high time for war," Seth muttered. "The British have never respected our American border. They interfere with our trade. And everyone says they encourage some of the Indian tribes to cause trouble."

"For years they've been kidnapping American sailors on the Atlantic Ocean and forcing them to join the British navy," Grandmother added.

"And now they've kidnapped Papa and Oliver," Caroline said. She slid one hand into her pocket and clenched the cord, now thick with Flemish knots, that Papa had given her.

Mama began to pace again. "I wish I had a way to

send a message to Aaron and Martha in Upper Canada, but now . . ." Her voice trailed away.

Caroline understood Mama's worry. Uncle Aaron and Aunt Martha, Oliver and Lydia's parents, had moved their family from New York to Upper Canada several years earlier.

"I can take a message to them," Seth offered.

Caroline's eyes widened. "Is it still safe for you to go to Upper Canada now that we're at war?"

"I have several letters that need to be delivered there," Seth said with determination. "People are depending on me. I'll make sure Lydia's safe at home with her parents."

"But you're an American," Caroline said. She turned to her mother. "If Seth goes to Canada, won't the British arrest him, too?"

"I don't think so," Mama replied. "*White Gull* attracted attention because it was flying an American flag."

"And because both sides are desperate for ships," Seth added. "People are saying that whichever side can control the Great Lakes will likely win the war."

"Still, we don't know what's happening over there."

Mama looked Seth in the eye. "We're grateful for your kindness, but you must be careful."

"I will," Seth promised. "I'll head northeast to the Saint Lawrence River. I know someone with a small fishing boat who can get me across. We won't fly any flag at all."

"Good luck," Caroline said. "And thank you."

Seth started toward the door, but then he turned back to Mrs. Abbott. "I almost forgot! I was at Porter's warehouse earlier. He said to tell you that the carpet you ordered arrived this morning. He'll have his men bring it around."

After Seth had left, Grandmother spoke. "It may be best to have Porter send the carpet back. That may be a luxury you can no longer afford." She looked at her granddaughter. "I'm sorry, Caroline. I know it was meant for your bedroom."

It took Caroline a moment to understand why Grandmother was concerned. Then she remembered that Papa had purchased the lumber and supplies needed to build *White Gull,* and the ship had been seized before Oliver could make even one trading trip and begin to pay Papa back. And now Papa and Oliver were prisoners, and no one knew how long they'd be held. How would Mama pay the bills? Would Abbott's Shipyard close? Would Mama have to sell their house? How would they even buy food?

"No." Mama put her hands on her hips. "We will keep the carpet. The British have done enough damage without denying my daughter a carpet to warm her feet this winter!" She looked so fierce that, in spite of everything, Caroline felt her lips curl in a tiny smile.

"Now, then," Mama continued. "Let's think about what must be done."

Grandmother leaned over and added another small log to the fire. "You need to see to the shipyard."

"And you could talk to the navy men in Sackets Harbor," Caroline suggested hopefully. "Lieutenant Woolsey, isn't that the man in charge? Maybe he'll launch a raid on Kingston and get Papa and Oliver back home."

Mama nodded. "You're both right. I'll go down to the shipyard first. I don't want the men wondering if they're about to lose their jobs." She whipped off her gardening apron and quickly scrubbed most of the mud from beneath her fingernails. "Caroline, stay here and help your grandmother. The carpet will be delivered this afternoon, and there's supper to fix."

"But I don't want—" Caroline began. Then she stopped. She didn't want to stay home and worry while Mama went to the shipyard. But she could still hear an echo of Papa's voice: *Stay steady, Caroline. Obey your mama. Give her and your grandmother whatever help they need while I'm away.*

Caroline thought about that, trying to decide what was best. Finally she said, "I can stay and help Grandmother, but I might also be able to help you at the shipyard. I know where Papa keeps his books, and I know all the men by name."

Grandmother nodded approvingly. "I'm fine here alone."

Mama paused, and then reached for her shawl. "Very well. Caroline, come with me."

Lieutenant Woolsey

aroline had to hurry to keep up with Mama as they headed out. Caroline was glad that her bossy neighbor wasn't in sight. Mrs. Shaw had once told Caroline's mother that Papa spent too much time with Caroline. "It's clear that Mr. Abbott adores his daughter," Mrs. Shaw had said, "but do you think it's wise to let Caroline spend so much time at the shipyard? A daughter's place is in the home, learning cooking and needlework."

"There are many girls twice her age who aren't as skilled at needlework," Mama had said crisply. At the time, Caroline had ignored Mrs. Shaw's comments. Today, she wasn't sure she'd be able to.

The village seemed to crackle with worried excitement. Passersby jostled Caroline as she and Mama made their way past homes and shops. A few warehouses stood nearer the water, filled with crates and barrels of goods—window glass, boots, china teapots, books, chocolate. The roads leading from Sackets Harbor to inland New York were narrow, rutted, and barely passable for much of the year. Almost all supplies came and went by ship.

Caroline felt a painful little lurch in her chest as they came to the wooden sign, painted with a graceful sloop, that simply said "Abbott's." An almost-finished schooner towered over their heads on a slipway— a narrow log bed near the water's edge from which the finished ship would be launched. The skeleton of another ship was rising up on heavy wooden support posts. Ladders leaned against the hull, and scraps of wood littered the ground. No carpenters were in sight, though. No one bustled past pushing a wheelbarrow or hauling lumber. No one shouted orders, or pounded with his hammer, or sang old songs.

They found Mr. Tate and a dozen other workers in the carpentry shop. Each man had a special skill. Some men worked with wood, some filled the seams between planks to make ships watertight, some prepared the ropes that sailors used to handle the sails.

The men fell silent as Mama and Caroline stepped into the shop.

"Good afternoon, gentlemen," Mama said. "I can see that you've already heard the sorry news."

Mr. Tate tugged the lock of hair that fell over his forehead, a sailor's traditional gesture of respect. "Forgive me if I spoke out of turn, Mrs. Abbott, but I felt the men should know."

"Of course." Mama took a deep breath and squared her shoulders. "I don't know how long my husband will be away. And I don't know what the war will mean for our business."

The men exchanged troubled glances. Then Hosea Barton, the sailmaker, stepped forward. His skin was as brown as mahogany, and Caroline had always loved to watch his strong, dark fingers working against the pale sailcloth. "Pardon me, ma'am," he said. "Are we out of work?"

"No, you are not," Mama said firmly. "Abbott's has promised to complete those two schooners outside, and we will not disappoint our customers. Mr. Tate, do you have everything you need to continue?"

"Why . . . yes, ma'am!"

"Good. You are in charge until Mr. Abbott returns."

Jed, the youngest woodworker, spoke up. "What happens if Mr. Abbott doesn't come back?"

"Papa *will* be back!" Caroline glared at Jed. The workshop went completely quiet. Jed flushed and looked at his shoes. For a moment the only sound was the noisy cries of gulls outside, fighting over fish scraps.

Then Mama looked Jed in the eye. "Of course Mr. Abbott will return," she said, quietly but firmly. "Now, you may all get back to work."

The men began heading to the door. Samuel, the ropemaker's apprentice, paused to say, "Thank you, ma'am. We'll do Mr. Abbott proud."

When the other men were gone, Mr. Tate shifted his weight uneasily from one foot to the other. "Mrs. Abbott," he began in a low voice, "I can manage the men. But there's the account books . . ."

"I kept the books when Mr. Abbott and I began the business," Mama said. "I can do so again."

Mr. Tate looked surprised and then relieved. "Yes, ma'am," he said.

Mama took Caroline's hand. "Come along. I need to look at Papa's business papers."

When Caroline reached the doorway of Papa's empty office, her feet stopped moving. The air still smelled of his spicy blend of pipe tobacco. The design drawings he'd made for the two schooners were tacked up on one wall. His favorite tankard sat on the desk. Caroline longed to blink and see Papa hard at work among his things. But he was not there.

Finally she followed Mama into the room. Mama touched a model of the first sloop Papa had ever built. Suddenly Caroline felt Mama shudder as she gulped down a sob.

For a moment Caroline wanted to cry, too. Instead she slipped her hand into her mother's. "You can keep the business going, Mama. I know you can. And . . . I can help you." She wasn't sure how, but she was determined to try.

Mama wiped her eyes and gave Caroline a watery smile. "You know where Papa keeps the ledger?"

"Yes. Right here." Caroline opened a wooden box on the desk and pulled out a leather-bound book. "Contracts for those two schooners are here, and he keeps bills in this drawer."

"Goodness," Mama said. "How fortunate that

you've spent so much time helping your father."

"But I don't know anything important," Caroline said sadly. "Sometimes I copied a bill or letter for Papa. Or I tidied up his office, or I read to the men as they worked. That's all." None of that would be of help now.

"I'll sort it out," Mama assured her. She squinted at the lines of Papa's slanting script. "I hope that—"

The door burst open. Caroline gave a little squeak of surprise as Lieutenant Woolsey himself stepped inside. He didn't look much older than Oliver, but he'd been stationed in Sackets Harbor for several years, enforcing trade laws and capturing smugglers. He had curly hair swept back from his face, and side-whiskers that stretched along his jaw. His blue uniform coat glittered with gold lace and buttons and braid.

Lieutenant Woolsey quickly pulled off his hat. "Are you Mrs. Abbott?"

"I am," Mama said. "And this is my daughter, Caroline. Thank you for coming so quickly."

Lieutenant Woolsey looked confused. "For coming quickly?"

"Aren't you here because of my husband?"

"Well, yes, ma'am. I have some business to discuss

with him." He tapped his leg impatiently. "With the news that war has been declared, that business is quite urgent. Is he here?"

"The British took him prisoner!" Caroline burst out. "And they stole our new sloop."

The lieutenant's eyebrows rose in surprise. "Mr. Abbott was sailing *White Gull*? I'd heard another name—Oliver Livingston."

"Oliver is my brother's son," Mama told him. "He was to captain the sloop. My daughter was there as well. Caroline, perhaps you should tell Lieutenant Woolsey what happened."

Caroline explained as quickly and clearly as she could. "So you see, sir," she concluded, "we need you to get Papa and Oliver back. And the sloop, too."

Lieutenant Woolsey rubbed his chin with one knuckle. He did not reply.

Caroline felt her heart grow heavier. "Won't you help us?" she asked. "Can't you send navy men to Kingston?"

He began turning his hat in his hands. "It's not that simple. I have no idea where the British have taken your father and cousin, and—"

"My Uncle Aaron could probably find out,"

Caroline said. She saw Mama's small frown and knew it was because she'd interrupted, but the words kept pouring out. "He and Aunt Martha and my cousin Lydia live in Upper Canada. If he can find out where the British are holding Papa and Oliver, will you go get them back? *Please?*"

Lieutenant Woolsey sighed. "I wish there were something I could do, but—"

"My husband was captured before news of the war had even reached us," Mama said sharply, "and you propose to do nothing?"

"On the contrary, ma'am, I am doing all I can," he retorted. "Now that war has been declared, keeping Lake Ontario safe for ships is of great importance to the United States. My first priority is to strengthen our defenses here against possible attack. I've already alerted our soldiers to be on guard."

Caroline's eyes widened. The British might attack Sackets Harbor?

"We need to build a fleet with all speed," the lieutenant was saying. "I've heard that Mr. Abbott is quite skilled."

"He is," Caroline said fiercely.

"We're starting a navy shipyard here. However, the workers haven't arrived yet." Lieutenant Woolsey shoved a hand through his hair. "Mrs. Abbott, I was going to ask your husband to build a gunboat for the navy. But now that he's been captured—"

"Nothing has changed," Mama said firmly. "Abbott's Shipyard still employs the finest craftsmen you could hope to find. I am managing the yard while my husband is away. And yes, we will build a gunboat for you."

Lieutenant Woolsey twisted his hat more forcefully. *He'll ruin that hat if he's not careful,* Caroline thought.

"Will your workers know what to do without Mr. Abbott?" he asked finally. "The British in Kingston are already at work on their own ships. We *must* not let them get ahead of us. Your men aren't used to building ships that can carry heavy cannons. Even the sails will be different, made of heavier cloth."

Caroline felt her impatience growing. "The men can build big ships! And Hosea Barton—he's our sailmaker—he's the best on the lakes!"

Mama put a hand on Caroline's shoulder and squeezed, as if to say, *That's enough, now.* Caroline pinched her lips together.

"I see," Lieutenant Woolsey said. The hat turned another circle in his hands.

"My daughter is correct, sir," Mama said. "Our workers can do whatever needs doing."

"Very well, then," the lieutenant said. "Do you have a lawyer? Someone whom your husband would trust to sign a contract?"

Mama's eyebrows rose. "My husband would trust *me*, sir. I will sign whatever documents are required. After I have reviewed them, of course, and we have agreed to whatever changes might be necessary. Draw them up and have them delivered here."

He nodded, made an attempt to smooth his hat, and planted it back on his head. "Thank you, Mrs. Abbott." He looked from Caroline to Mama. "I *am* sorry about what happened today, but I suspect you'll get good news soon. Your men were not members of the military, nor smugglers. I'm sure that the British will release them."

"When?" Caroline demanded. "Today?"

"Well, perhaps not today," he said. "I'm afraid you must simply be patient and wait." With that, Lieutenant Woolsey walked out the door.

Grandmother's Advice

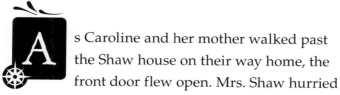s Caroline and her mother walked past the Shaw house on their way home, the front door flew open. Mrs. Shaw hurried down the gravel path and crushed Caroline into a hug. "Oh, you poor, poor child."

Her pity didn't make Caroline feel any better. Mrs. Shaw was a plump woman, with a round face that Caroline thought only *looked* kind. She wriggled free from her neighbor's arms.

"Lieutenant Woolsey believes the British will release my husband soon," Mama said.

"He knows best," Mrs. Shaw replied.

"Perhaps." Mama frowned. "Actually, though, I think Lieutenant Woolsey is too busy right now to worry about Mr. Abbott and Oliver."

"Well, he has many things to worry about."

Mrs. Shaw spread her hands. "We all have much to do to prepare for war. My husband volunteers with the gun crew, you know. Thank heavens they've been practicing."

"Lieutenant Woolsey said Sackets Harbor is poorly defended," Caroline said. Remembering the grim look on the officer's face made her shiver.

"If so, it's not the gun crew's fault," Mrs. Shaw huffed. "The government sent cannonballs that don't even fit their cannons."

"The cannonballs don't fit?" Caroline echoed. "How can we defend ourselves?"

"We must pray that our soldiers find a solution." Mama pressed her lips together. "Now, Mrs. Shaw, if you will excuse us, Caroline and I should get home."

Mrs. Shaw put a hand on Mama's arm. "What will happen to the shipyard?"

"Mama is taking charge until Papa gets back," Caroline told her.

Mrs. Shaw looked at Mama. "I can't imagine how you'll manage the shipyard *and* your household!"

"I'm going to help," Caroline said. Couldn't Mrs. Shaw tell that she was only making Mama feel worse?

Mrs. Shaw patted Caroline's shoulder. "I'm sure you mean well, Caroline. But we all know that your kitchen skills are a bit, well . . . lacking."

Caroline flushed. Two days earlier, Mrs. Shaw had stopped by just as Caroline was taking bread out of the bake oven. Grandmother was teaching Caroline how to bake, but somehow, Caroline never seemed able to mix in just the right amount of flour and water, or knead the dough to the perfect silky-smooth texture. Her loaf had turned out heavy and hard.

Now Mama said sharply, "Mrs. Shaw!"

"I don't mean to criticize," Mrs. Shaw said, although Caroline was sure that was *exactly* what she meant to do. "We must all pull together in times like these," the older woman added. "I'd be glad to help teach Caroline."

Oh no, Caroline thought. Her spirits sank lower.

"Thank you for the offer," Mama said. "But we'll do fine. Good afternoon." Caroline and Mama walked the rest of the way in silence.

Once they were home, Caroline let Mama tell Grandmother about the conversation with Lieutenant

Woolsey. Caroline plodded up the stairs.

When Caroline reached her small bedroom, she caught her breath. Her carpet had been delivered! Last March, Mama had taken Caroline to look at samples. "Pick out exactly what you want," Mama had said. It was the first time her parents had ever permitted Caroline to make such an important, grown-up decision. She had looked at each sample carefully, feeling the materials and trying to imagine how such a carpet would look in her bedroom. It had been so hard to choose!

Now Caroline knew her choice was perfect. The new carpet was made of thick wool in warm shades of gold and brown. The beautiful carpet, soft and cozy, would make her unheated room feel warmer during Sackets Harbor's icy winters. Even now, on a day when everything had gone so terribly wrong, the carpet was comforting.

Inkpot, her black cat, must have found the carpet comforting, too. He was curled into a ball in a patch of sunlight, fast asleep. Caroline scooped him up and nestled one cheek against his soft fur. Papa had brought Inkpot home when he was no more than a scruffy stray kitten. "Sailors believe black cats are good luck," he'd told Caroline.

"I wish you'd been on board *White Gull* today," Caroline whispered. "Maybe you would have brought us better luck." Inkpot purred sleepily, and Caroline gently put him down again.

She walked to the little mahogany worktable in the corner. The table had a hinged board where she could write letters, and compartments for bottles of ink and notepaper and blotting sand. A lower drawer had plenty of space for her sewing supplies. A fabric bag slung beneath the worktable held her current project, an embroidered map of Lake Ontario's eastern shoreline from Sackets Harbor around to Kingston.

In an instant, all the pleasure Caroline had taken in her new carpet faded. She'd planned to put the map, when it was finished, into a wooden frame so that Papa could use it as a fire screen. She had loved imagining Papa sitting in his favorite chair by the hearth on frosty winter nights, with the fire screen allowing him to stay warm without getting scorched. When the lake was iced over and Papa couldn't sail, the embroidered map would remind him that spring would come again.

Now Papa was gone, and his fate was unknown. *Will Papa ever even see the map?* Caroline wondered miserably.

She turned and clattered back down the stairs, across the hall, and out the front door. She didn't stop running until Lake Ontario spread below her. To the west, the lake stretched toward a horizon stained pink and orange by the setting sun. Caroline stared in the direction of Kingston. Papa and Oliver were out there, *somewhere*. Had the British put them in jail? Did they have enough to eat? When would they be coming home? The ache in her heart threatened to take her breath away.

The lake was darkening to black when, sometime later, Caroline heard footsteps. "I roasted some white-fish," Grandmother said as she joined Caroline. "And baked gingerbread."

"I'm not hungry," Caroline told her.

Grandmother planted her cane in front of her and rested both hands on it. "I don't imagine you are," she said. "But you can't fight the British if you don't eat."

"*I* can't fight the British!" Caroline protested. She hated feeling so angry—and so helpless.

"No, but you can help me tend the house."

Caroline blinked away tears. "I can't even bake bread that's fit to eat."

To her surprise, Grandmother chuckled. "All you need is practice."

Caroline didn't want to practice baking bread, and she didn't want to be at war. "I want things to be as they were this morning," she said.

Grandmother shook her head. "I'm afraid such thoughts are a waste of time, my girl."

I can't help it, Caroline thought. One more protest slipped out: "What happened today just isn't *fair.*"

"Life often isn't fair," Grandmother said. "We can turn bitter and complain about our problems. Or we can try to change what we may, and make the best of every day we're given."

For a long moment Caroline and Grandmother stood in silence, watching spots of light blink from the village as swallows swooped overhead. Then Caroline said, "I disappointed Papa today. He told me I was too flighty."

"I see," Grandmother said. She sounded thoughtful.

"I wanted to show him that I can do better," Caroline

said miserably. "But now the British have taken him! What if I never get the chance?"

"I believe you will," Grandmother said. "But Caroline, think for a moment. I suspect your papa was asking you to be more responsible. That's good advice, whether he's home or not. With your mother working at the shipyard, I'll need more help from you here at home."

Scrubbing floors and weeding gardens won't help bring Papa and Oliver home, Caroline thought. She wanted to do something that would help get them back! But she knew that Grandmother, with all her aches and pains, couldn't manage the house alone.

Caroline looked at the woman standing beside her. "Grandmother? How did you manage during the Revolution?" With a shiver, she remembered what Lieutenant Woolsey had said about a possible British attack on Sackets Harbor. "Were you ever in the middle of the fighting?"

"Once," Grandmother said.

"Weren't you scared?"

Grandmother stared into the growing shadows. "I was taking water to my husband and his men.

I knew how desperately they needed it, and so . . .
I went. I wasn't afraid until later."

"It must have been horrible when Grandfather got killed," Caroline whispered. Those events had always seemed like something from the very distant past to her. Suddenly, they seemed much more real.

"It *was* horrible," Grandmother agreed. "But I had a farm to tend and children to raise. I learned that women can do what they must."

"I'll do my best to help you and Mama," Caroline promised. "But I wish I could do something to help Papa, too. To help fight the British."

"More than anything else, I think, your papa would want you to stay safe," Grandmother said. "Far away from the British."

Caroline would be grateful if she never saw a British uniform again! But staying away from the British wouldn't help Papa, either. She sighed. "I don't want your bones to get chilled," she told her grandmother. "Let's go back inside."

Attack!

Six days later, Seth returned. He had traveled to Upper Canada and back. "Lydia is safe at home," he reported. "Her father is trying to find out where Mr. Abbott and Oliver are being held."

"I'll give Mrs. Abbott the news as soon as she returns from the shipyard," Grandmother said. She and Caroline were sitting in the kitchen, watching Seth gobble warm biscuits and honey. "What's the situation over there?"

"Everything is upside down." Seth caught a drop of honey and licked it from his finger. "People in Upper Canada are terrified that Americans are going to invade. No one knows whether they should hunker down or run for their lives."

"The same thing is happening here," Caroline told him. "Some people have left already." She worked

another stitch on her embroidery, pulling the silk
thread carefully so that it didn't tangle. Caroline had
found that whenever worry threatened to overwhelm
her, it helped to keep her hands busy.

Seth finished a third biscuit and got to his feet.
"Please excuse me, but I've got a long way to walk
yet today."

"Thank you for bringing us news," Caroline
told him.

"I was glad to," Seth said. "And Caroline? Try
not to worry too much. Your father will likely come
home soon."

Caroline wanted to believe her friend. But days
inched by, and then weeks. June turned into July. And
Papa did not come home.

Every day Caroline's neighbors grew more fearful
of a British invasion. And every day Caroline's worry
for her father and Oliver was pulled tighter, like a knotted piece of embroidery silk. Uncle Aaron managed to
send a letter across the lake in a fishing boat. He wrote
that Oliver and Papa were being held in the fort that

the British were constructing at Kingston. No one knew how long the two would be kept as prisoners.

Sometimes Caroline went to the shipyard with Mama, where the men were already at work on Lieutenant Woolsey's new gunboat. Sometimes Caroline stayed home with Grandmother, where the garden grew as many weeds as beans and carrots. Always, though, she was waiting for her father—for a glimpse of him hurrying up the hill, for his shout of greeting, for his Papa-scent of tobacco and sawdust, for the feel of his strong hands squeezing hers as if to say, *Well done, Caroline. I'm proud of you.*

One Sunday morning in late July, Caroline took a basket to the garden. A traveling minister was visiting the village, and Grandmother had asked her to pick the ripe peas before they left for the service. Mama had already headed to the shipyard, where the crew was working seven days a week.

As Caroline snapped the first pod from the vine, a *boom* shuddered through the hot morning. "I suppose the gun crew wants to get their practice in before church, too," she told Inkpot, who was chasing crickets nearby.

Then she heard someone yelling, "Miss Caroline!
Miss Caroline!" Samuel, the apprentice ropemaker,
burst through the garden gate. His shirt was damp
with sweat.

Caroline scrambled to her feet. "What's wrong?"
she cried.

"They're coming!" Samuel gasped. He bent over,
hands on knees, trying to catch his breath.

Caroline's heart took a hopeful leap. "Papa and
Oliver?"

"The *British*!" Another thundering *boom* almost
drowned out Samuel's words. "That's the alarm guns,
calling in the militia."

Caroline lifted her skirt and ran across the lane
toward the lake. "Oh," she gasped. Five ships flying
the flag of Great Britain had formed a ragged line and
trapped the American ship *Oneida* inside the harbor.

Caroline's hands curled into fists. "If the British
take *Oneida*, we won't have any big ships left to
protect us!"

Samuel had followed her. "Lieutenant Woolsey
tried to sail *Oneida* out of the harbor," he said, "but the
British ships cut him off."

Grandmother hobbled up to join them. "Have mercy," she muttered.

"Mrs. Abbott said you're both to hide in the root cellar," Samuel told them.

"What about Mama?" Caroline cried, but Samuel was already loping away.

"Your mama's place is at the shipyard," said Grandmother. "If the British do make land, they'll look for shipbuilding tools and supplies. What they can't carry off, they'll want to burn."

When Caroline imagined British sailors plundering Abbott's Shipyard, she tasted something sour in her throat. A cannon on one of the British ships fired. The noise shivered through the morning. A plume of gray smoke rose from the gun.

Caroline grabbed Grandmother's hand. "We've got to get to the root cellar before a cannonball lands on us! Come along. I'll help you."

Before they'd taken two steps, though, Mrs. Shaw's shrill voice sliced through the air. "Caroline! Mrs. Livingston! I . . . need your . . . help!" she gasped, stumbling across the yard to meet them. Her straw bonnet was dangling by its strings. Dust and sweat streaked her best Sunday dress.

"What's wrong?" Caroline cried.

"My husband's gun crew—the cannonballs they have are too small!" Mrs. Shaw's shoulders were still heaving with the effort of running. "Our men need heavy cloth to wrap around them so they'll fit the cannons."

"Caroline, fetch my winter cloak," Grandmother said.

"Grandmother, no," Caroline protested. It was the warmest thing she owned.

"Fetch it now!" Grandmother ordered. "And your own, and your mother's. *Quickly.*"

Caroline blinked back tears as she ran to the house. Fear made her legs feel wobbly and her mouth feel as dry as cotton. But she was also angry. Grandmother would suffer terribly next winter without her thick wool cloak.

By the time Caroline pounded up the stairs, her anger felt as hot as coals. She skidded to a stop at her bedroom door, staring at her new carpet as an idea burst into her mind. *Maybe my carpet could be used to wrap the cannonballs!* she thought. Maybe Grandmother wouldn't have to lose her cloak after all.

Caroline turned and ran downstairs. "Mrs. Shaw!" she hollered. "Come help me! Grandmother, can you fetch the wheelbarrow from the garden?"

It took all the strength Caroline and Mrs. Shaw had between them to roll up Caroline's new carpet. They slid the bulky roll down the stairs and wrestled it into the wheelbarrow. The two ends flopped over the sides and dragged in the dirt.

It hurt Caroline's heart to see her beautiful carpet used so roughly. *This is the right thing to do*, she told herself sternly. She squared her shoulders and grasped the wheelbarrow's handles. A gun boomed and Caroline glanced at Grandmother. *If we go*, she thought, *Grandmother will be left to face the attacks alone.* Caroline hesitated, torn between wanting to protect her grandmother and wanting to help the gun crew.

Grandmother seemed to understand. "Go!" she said. "I'll be fine."

Mrs. Shaw was struggling with the carpet. "Caroline, let's fold the roll over like this. If I hold it in place, can you push?"

Another shot exploded from one of the enemy ships

as Caroline lifted the wheelbarrow handles and stag-
gered off. She pushed until her hands and arms ached,
and then she and Mrs. Shaw traded places. *Hurry,
hurry, hurry,* Caroline urged silently, but there was no
need to encourage Mrs. Shaw. Caroline could never
have imagined her fussy neighbor so grim-faced and
determined. *But then I never could have imagined heading
for the gun crew while the British fired at Sackets Harbor,
either,* she thought.

It was hard going. Groups of militiamen elbowed
past—farmers and workmen who had promised to
grab their muskets and report for duty when trouble
threatened. Someone on a horse galloped by. A woman
led a string of children, all lugging bundles and baskets,
toward the woods.

Caroline and Mrs. Shaw stumbled past the harbor
and on toward the cannons. Sweat rolled into Caroline's
eyes. Her back ached. The trip seemed to take forever.

Then Caroline heard men shouting, just ahead.
She looked up and saw Lieutenant Woolsey yelling
orders to a dozen men scrambling around several
cannons. Scraps of cloth—probably someone else's
winter cloak—lay on the ground nearby.

"We need help!" Mrs. Shaw shrieked. She dropped the wheelbarrow handles with a little moan and rubbed her hands. Several men ran to help.

Caroline straightened her back and lifted one edge of the carpet. "Will it suit?" she cried.

"I surely hope so," Mr. Shaw said grimly. "Everything we've tried has either been too thick or too thin. The cannon won't fire if the ball doesn't fit snug inside."

Another man reached for the knife slung into his belt. He slashed a ragged square from the carpet with a harsh tearing sound. Caroline held her breath as the men carefully wrapped one of their cannonballs with the carpet. They held the strange package against the cannon's mouth, checking the size.

"Hurrah!" a gunner cried. Several others cheered.

"It suits?" Caroline asked again.

Mr. Shaw nodded, red-faced and sweaty. "It's perfect!"

Mrs. Shaw grabbed Caroline's hand and pulled her a short distance away.

"May we stay and watch?" Caroline begged.

"Just for a moment," Mrs. Shaw said. She seemed to understand how Caroline felt.

One of the gunners began shouting orders. "Load! Ram home charge! Prime!" Caroline didn't understand all the words, but the gun crew did. Each man had a special job to do as the cannon was readied. *It's almost like watching a dance,* Caroline thought, *where everyone knows the steps.*

"Ready!" the man yelled. A man holding a burning stick stepped forward to light the gunpowder. *"Fire!"*

The cannon boomed. Caroline jumped and clapped her hands over her ears. A sharp smell stung her nose. A cloud of gray smoke appeared.

"Drive them off, boys!" Mrs. Shaw shouted.

"Yes!" Caroline cried. "Drive them off!" Mrs. Shaw grinned at her. Caroline grinned back.

The gun crew didn't waste time cheering. The men were already getting new orders. Step by step, they prepared the cannon to fire again.

Mrs. Shaw took Caroline's hand once more. "We must get back home," she said. "Your grandmother will be worried."

Caroline realized that in her excitement, she had almost forgotten the danger they were in. "Yes," she agreed. "We should go."

Mrs. Shaw held Caroline's hand all the way home. Caroline didn't mind a bit.

"I am so proud of you." Mama put both hands on Caroline's shoulders. "What a clever girl you are! Taking the carpet to the gun crew must have been terribly frightening."

It was late afternoon. The fighting was over. Mama had invited all the shipyard workers home for a picnic supper, and now they sprawled on the lawn. Hosea and Samuel had built a fire and were preparing to roast some trout. Grandmother brought out cornbread and a raspberry cobbler.

Mama's praise made Caroline feel warm inside. "I wasn't frightened until later," she confessed, glancing at Grandmother. "I just wanted to help win the battle."

"And, by heaven, those cannonballs ran the British off!" Mr. Tate said.

Lieutenant Woolsey's men had exchanged fire with the British ships for about two hours. At the shipyard, the men had prepared for a fight, arming themselves with clubs and hammers. Mama had stood with Papa's pistol in her hand, ready to defend the yard. But the British had suddenly lifted anchor and sailed back toward Kingston without landing at all. The American ships in Sackets Harbor were safe.

Mama shook her head. "I was determined that the British would not deny you a carpet to warm your feet this winter," she said. "They did indeed cost you your carpet, but it was a sacrifice well worth making."

Mrs. Shaw, who had come to the celebration with her husband, smiled at Caroline. "We did well, didn't we?"

"We did," Caroline agreed. "We did indeed."

As one of the workers began to tell—for the third time—how he'd climbed to the roof of a shed, ready to drop down on the first British soldier to set foot into the shipyard, Caroline excused herself and walked to her favorite spot overlooking the lake.

So much had happened since the day Papa and Oliver had been taken prisoner! That day she'd stood on this very spot, feeling lost and helpless. Caroline missed Papa and Oliver as much as ever, but she felt a little more hopeful today. She felt proud, too. She'd been able to help the American cause.

Lake Ontario rippled in shades of blue and green below. Caroline could see *Oneida* patrolling nearby. There were no British ships in sight.

"We beat you," Caroline whispered. She knew the war was just beginning. The British would likely come again. But right now, she simply wanted to enjoy her small triumph. "We *beat* you," she said again, staring in the direction of Kingston. "And Papa, wherever you are . . . I'm trying to stay steady and ride out the storm. I'll never stop watching and waiting. And somehow, I'll help find a way to bring you back home."

It was a promise.

Home Again

CHAPTER 7

October 1812

All through the summer, Caroline tried her best to stay steady. She helped Grandmother at home and Mama at the shipyard, and always she watched and waited for Papa.

Now the weather was growing steadily colder, and everyone was busy with harvest chores. Caroline was picking pumpkins for Grandmother. She could see Mrs. Shaw busy in her garden, too.

Caroline cut the last pumpkin from its vine and straightened, resting her tired back. She blew out a frosty breath as she glanced at the pile of pumpkins she'd stacked by the side of the garden. *Grandmother will make good use of them this winter,* she thought. She could almost smell pumpkin pie fresh from the oven, scented with cinnamon and nutmeg.

Her heart caught. *Surely* Papa would be home by

winter . . . wouldn't he? Then Caroline pushed the question away. Worrying wouldn't bring Papa back.

Caroline hoisted the muddy pumpkin into her arms and headed inside, shivering as she kicked the kitchen door closed behind her. She eased the pumpkin to the floor. "Here's one to cook today," she told Grandmother. "I'll put the rest in the root cellar."

"Good," Grandmother said. "My bones tell me that a hard freeze is coming." From her chair near the fire, she leaned forward to stir the bean pot.

Caroline rubbed her hands on her apron. *It's bad enough that we're fighting the British,* she thought. Now the coming winter made her feel as if a second enemy was creeping close, ready to pounce.

"Perhaps Mama can stay home from the shipyard tomorrow," she said, "and help us handle the harvest."

"It's not easy for your mother to manage the ship-yard without your father," Grandmother said. "Back during the Revolution, I held my farm together with your mama's help. You and I can manage here now."

"Of course we can," Caroline said quickly. She didn't want Grandmother to think she was complaining! "I'll get back to work."

Caroline snugged her shawl against the October chill and went back to the muddy garden.

After hauling the pumpkins to the root cellar, Caroline grabbed a shovel. *Next, the potatoes,* she thought. She sat the shovel upright beside the mound of earth that held the first potato plant. Then she jumped onto the blade edge with both feet.

As she teetered there, using her weight to shove the blade beneath the buried potatoes, a whistle shrilled behind her. She lost her balance and tumbled to the ground. "Ow!"

"Oh, pardon me!" Her friend Seth Whittleslee leaned on the garden gate. His eyes danced with mischief. "Did I startle you?"

Caroline scrambled to her feet, slapping at the mud on her skirt. "Seth, that was unkind," she scolded. She couldn't stay annoyed with her good friend, though. His visits were too rare.

"Can you stay for supper?" she added hopefully. With Papa gone, having Seth at the table would make the meal seem less lonely.

"You're inviting me to stay for supper?" Seth asked, pretending to be surprised. "Why, how very kind."

Caroline snorted. Seth was skinny as a fence post from walking so many miles to deliver mail, and his appetite was famous. "Grandmother's making ginger cakes," Caroline said with a smile.

"I love your grandmother's ginger cakes!" Seth said. Then his grin faded. "Have you had any news about your father and Oliver?"

Caroline kicked a rock. "No," she said. "My birthday's in three weeks, and I *so* hope that Papa will be home by then. But we've had no news from him or Oliver. And we haven't heard from Oliver's parents in weeks, either."

"I haven't crossed to Canada in a while," Seth said. "Since the war began, most of my customers there have moved away."

Caroline stared over the garden fence. Soldiers had cut many trees as they built blockhouses and log walls to protect the village. Beyond the stumps, the forest was a flaming glory of cardinal red and egg-yolk yellow. She was too worried to enjoy the scene, though. "I wish I could just sail across the lake and find out what's happening!" she exclaimed. The thought of traveling to Upper Canada—maybe even to Kingston, where the British troops were headquartered—made her feel like custard, all quivery. But if she might learn something about Papa and Oliver, or perhaps even see them, she'd make the trip.

"You're running out of time then," Seth said. "It's getting cold for lake travel." He picked up the shovel, pushed it into the hole she'd started, and gave one good heave. The entire plant and all the potatoes clinging to its roots flipped free from the soil.

Caroline stooped and began gathering the potatoes into a basket. "Mama wants to go, too," she told him. "But since she's managing the shipyard now, she's worried about leaving the business."

"This war is a devil of a thing," Seth said grimly. "We won independence from the British thirty years ago. Shouldn't have to fight 'em again."

"Grandmother says it's a waste of time to talk about what can't be changed," Caroline told him. "She says, 'Find something you *can* do to help the situation.'" Caroline sighed. "That isn't always easy to do."

The war had brought many changes to Caroline's family and neighbors. In just a few months, their tiny village had become a bustling port. Abbott's Shipyard was building a small gunboat to carry troops and cannons. Shipwrights at the new navy shipyard nearby were working on a huge warship to fight the British on Lake Ontario. More sailors and carpenters arrived in town every day.

And people keep arriving, Caroline thought. As she picked up the heavy basket, she noticed another new-comer trudging up the lane. Caroline started to turn toward the root cellar, but something made her pause. She squinted at the young man approaching . . . and then she squealed with joy.

"Oliver! It's *Oliver*!" she cried. Surely Papa would be with him! She dropped the potatoes, lifted her skirt, and raced to meet her cousin. She wrapped him in a hug. His wool coat smelled of sweat and smoke. She didn't know whether to laugh or cry with happiness.

"Oh, Oliver—it's so good to see you!" she said finally, stepping back to drink in the sight of him. Instead of looking happy, though, Oliver looked serious.

Then Caroline realized that the lane behind her cousin was empty. "But—where's Papa?"

Oliver crouched down and took her hands. His face was thin and stubbly with a beard. His eyes were full of shadows. "Your papa isn't with me," he said. "I'm so sorry, Caroline. Two weeks ago the British put me on a boat, sailed me to the American side of the lake, and dropped me off on shore. I was miles from nowhere, and I've been making my way to Sackets Harbor ever since. But they didn't release your father."

Caroline stared at her cousin. She had always imagined Oliver and Papa being set free *together*. But here was Oliver, weary, skinny . . . and alone.

"Why wasn't Papa released?" Caroline asked as Grandmother and Seth joined them.

"Someone told the British that he is a master ship-builder," Oliver said. "The British asked him to work for them. He refused."

"I'd think so!" Seth muttered.

Oliver sighed. "But now they're holding him so that he can't come home and build ships for the American navy."

Caroline's shoulders slumped. Did that mean the British would keep Papa prisoner for the rest of the war? The war might last for years!

Oliver rose to his feet, wobbled a bit, and took a step to steady himself. Grandmother put one hand on his cheek, as if to be sure he was truly there. Her expression was hard, but her voice was gentle. "Welcome home, Oliver. Come along to the house. You need a good meal, a hot bath, and a soft bed."

Oliver looked back at Caroline. He seemed to be waiting for something.

"Welcome home," Caroline echoed. "We're very glad you're here." And it was true—she was so glad to see her cousin again! But her heart still felt heavy as an anchor.

By late afternoon, the Abbotts' kitchen was fragrant with fresh biscuits, baked beans, and potatoes fried with chopped onions. Caroline collected pewter plates and set them on the sturdy table. Ever since Papa had been taken prisoner, she and Mama and Grandmother had eaten every meal in the kitchen. It was comforting to eat near the hearth, with her cat, Inkpot, purring on the braided rug.

She poured mugs of cider for Oliver and Seth. A bath, a nap, and clean clothes had clearly done Oliver good.

"I'm feeling better already," he said. "And I've made a decision. I intend to join the navy."

"But—you just got home!" Caroline protested.

Grandmother's eyes filled with sadness, but she nodded. "I'm proud of you, Oliver."

Caroline looked at her cousin. *He needs our help now,* she thought. "I'm proud of you, too," she whispered.

"Thank you," Oliver said. "It feels so good to be free and to make my own decisions!" Then he sighed. "I'm just sorry the British didn't release Uncle John with me."

Mama drew in a long breath and blew it out again. "That isn't your fault," she told Oliver firmly. "Tonight we will celebrate *your* safe return."

Oliver took a long drink of cider and wiped his mouth with his hand. "There's something else you need to know."

Caroline clenched her hands together in her lap. *Is there more bad news?* she wondered.

"The British have more prisoners than they can handle in Kingston," Oliver said. He glanced at Caroline and then away. "They're planning to send most of them east."

"East!" Caroline cried. "Where?"

Oliver's jaw tightened. "Halifax."

Halifax? Caroline didn't know exactly where Halifax was, but she knew it was far away—all the way to the Atlantic coast.

Trying to ease the sudden pounding of her heart, Caroline got up and reached for her sewing, which she had set on a bench by the fire. Concentrating on her embroidery stitches, she busied her hands and listened to the talk.

"Winter is coming . . . and now this," Mama said grimly. "I can't wait any longer to take action."

Caroline looked up. "We're going to Canada?" she asked hopefully. Perhaps she would see Papa soon after all!

Mama corrected her. "*I* am going to Canada."

Caroline wanted to protest. She longed to see Papa, too! But in her mind, she heard his voice: *I need you to stay steady, Caroline. Obey your mama.* Quickly she looked back down at her work, biting her lip and forcing herself to make perfectly neat, even stitches.

"I will not let the British take my husband to some distant prison without trying to see him," Mama was saying. "Perhaps I can even convince the British officers to release him."

Caroline felt her spirits rise just a little. When the British had tried to capture Sackets Harbor, Mama had stood with Papa's pistol in her hand, ready to defend the shipyard. If anyone could convince the British to release Papa, it was Mama.

"I should be able to sail to Upper Canada in a day," Mama said. "Oliver, I'll let your parents know you are safe and well. I can spend the night at their farm before going on to Kingston."

"Can you handle the skiff by yourself?" Oliver asked. He sounded worried.

Caroline thought about how windy it could be on Lake Ontario. Mama was an experienced sailor, but it would take a lot of strength to sail all the way to Upper Canada. Papa mostly used the little skiff, named *Sparrow,* for fishing in sheltered waters near Sackets Harbor. Kingston, though, was thirty miles away! And storms could blow in quickly on the lake. Oliver was right to worry.

"I'll watch the weather and stay close to shore," Mama promised. "I can always stop to rest or take shelter at the Baxter place."

"No!" Seth said sharply. Then he lowered his voice. "The Baxters are loyal to Great Britain. It wouldn't be safe to stop there."

Caroline felt a sinking sensation in her chest. The Baxters were old family friends who had started a farm on an island just across the border. The Abbotts had often stopped there on visits to Upper Canada. *It's terrible to think that Mama wouldn't be safe with the Baxters,* Caroline thought. She stitched faster, pushing back her fear as she pushed the needle through the cloth.

"This could be a dangerous trip for more reasons than one," Oliver reminded Mama. "I'll go with you. I can help with the skiff, and I'm eager to see my family before I enlist."

Grandmother banged her mug on the table, making everyone jump. "Don't be foolish," she told Oliver. "The British arrested you on an American ship once. If anyone were to spot you in Upper Canada again, you'd be off to Halifax, too."

"I'm willing to take that risk," Oliver insisted. "I can't just sit here while Uncle John is still being held. The British will never let him come home to build ships for the American navy." He lowered his voice, as if worried that a British soldier might be listening. "Uncle John needs to escape."

"You think Papa might be able to *escape*?" Caroline asked. Sometimes her heart felt like a skiff caught in a windy squall, blown back and forth between hope and despair.

"It wouldn't be easy," Oliver said quickly. "But I've heard about several prisoners who escaped from boats headed for Halifax. A prisoner can quickly slip away and hide in the woods along the Saint Lawrence River." Oliver raked his fingers through his hair. "If I go back, perhaps I could somehow help Uncle John—"

"And who will help *you* escape when you're captured for a second time?" Grandmother demanded. "Not one more word from you about traveling to Kingston."

Oliver looked as if he wanted to argue. Then he reluctantly nodded.

"Mama," Caroline said, "if you *are* allowed to see Papa, perhaps you can whisper to him! Tell him that if the British send him east, that will be his best chance to escape!"

Seth looked at Mama. "The skiff will be easier to handle with a second person along. I'd be glad to escort you, Mrs. Abbott," he offered.

"I can't let you take that risk," Mama said. "My husband is a prisoner. If the British see you with me, they might decide you're in Upper Canada to cause trouble."

"How about taking one of the shipyard workers?" Caroline suggested.

Mama shook her head. "Every man is needed at the yard if the gunboat is to be built on time. Besides, British soldiers will be less suspicious of a woman traveler."

Caroline glanced around the table. Seth and Oliver looked worried. Mama looked determined. And Grandmother . . . Grandmother was looking intently at *her,* and there seemed to be a message in her eyes.

Suddenly Caroline understood. *Why, Grandmother thinks* I *should go.* Caroline caught her breath, her needle poised in midstitch. She wasn't as strong as Oliver or Seth, but she could help handle the skiff. Papa had taught her well. Caroline knew the trip would be much safer with two people.

She pulled her thread through the linen and took a deep breath. "You shouldn't travel alone, Mama," she said. "Please let me come with you."

Mama hesitated. "Very well, Caroline," she said finally. "You may come."

The Hathaways

ater that evening, after Seth had left, Caroline, Mama, and Grandmother made plans for the journey.

"If the weather is fair, we'll leave in the morning," Mama said.

Caroline smiled, but her stomach did a nervous flip-flop. She and Mama were going to see Papa! Still, the idea of going to Kingston made her anxious.

Suddenly a look of doubt crossed Mama's face. She looked from Caroline to Grandmother. "Perhaps I spoke in haste when I agreed to let Caroline come."

Caroline stared at Mama. "But—"

"I hope you're not thinking to leave her home on my account," Grandmother said sharply.

A log popped and snapped on the fire. Caroline chewed her lip, troubled with fresh worries.

Grandmother was a brave woman, but she moved slowly these days. With Oliver joining the navy, could she handle all of the harvesttime chores alone?

A knock on the front door startled everyone. "I'll answer it," Caroline said, tucking her embroidery into her apron pocket.

When Caroline opened the door, she was surprised to see three strangers: a woman, a girl who looked slightly older than Caroline, and a little girl. An American soldier stood behind them.

Caroline could see weariness in the slope of the woman's shoulders, in the older girl's downcast gaze, in the forlorn way the child leaned against her sister. A few snowflakes dotted their cloaks and the woman's travel bag.

"Is this the Abbott house?" the woman asked.

"Yes," Caroline said. "Please come in."

Mama's heels clicked on the hall floor behind her. "Good evening," she said. "I'm Mrs. Abbott. This is my daughter, Caroline."

The woman pushed back the hood of her cloak. She had brown hair and a thin face and wore narrow spectacles. "I'm Mrs. Hathaway," she said. "These are *my* daughters. The little one is Amelia, and this is Rhonda."

Rhonda was a few inches taller than Caroline, and she wore her auburn hair fixed in a fancy style. She smiled shyly as she pulled off her wool mittens.

Mrs. Hathaway adjusted her spectacles. "My husband is an army officer. We've traveled from Albany with his regiment, and I've spent the last hour looking for lodging. Most people are already full up with boarders."

No wonder the girls look tired, Caroline thought.

"Even a small space would be welcome," added Mrs. Hathaway. "We sometimes slept in a tent on our journey. We're quite used to making do."

Caroline and Mama exchanged a glance, and Caroline could tell that they were both thinking the same thing. "We have plenty of room," Caroline said.

Mrs. Hathaway smiled with relief. "You may report back to my husband," she told the soldier who had escorted her and the girls. "We've found a place to stay."

Oliver offered to sleep in the kitchen, leaving the spare bedroom for the Hathaways. Mrs. Hathaway and Amelia, who was four, would sleep in the bed. Mama helped Rhonda make a pallet on the floor with coverlets and blankets. "We'll make a cornhusk mattress for you, too," Mama assured Rhonda.

"We're grateful for your hospitality," Mrs. Hathaway declared. "In addition to paying for room and board, I'll be glad to help with chores."

Mama looked thoughtful. "Mrs. Hathaway, Caroline and I will be traveling for a few days. We hope to leave tomorrow."

"Grandmother is used to doing all the cooking," Caroline added. "Still, Mama and I are worried about leaving her alone."

"Worry no longer," Mrs. Hathaway said briskly. "Now, it's Amelia's bedtime."

"Come downstairs when you get her settled, and we'll have hot tea waiting," Mama promised. "Caroline, why don't you and Rhonda get acquainted?"

Caroline's eyes widened as Rhonda removed her cloak and bonnet. Her flowing, high-waisted green gown was trimmed with lace the color of eggshells.

She looked elegant! Caroline glanced from Mama's sturdy work dress to her own skirt, which was splattered with mud from the garden. Had Rhonda worn that fine dress for long days of rough travel?

"Caroline?" Mama prompted.

Caroline's cheeks grew hot. "I'll show you my bedchamber, Rhonda," she said.

Caroline led Rhonda to her room. It was small and narrow, but Caroline loved having a space of her own. Best of all, it faced north, so Caroline could sit by her window and see the water.

Rhonda's gaze settled on a mahogany worktable. "That's pretty."

"Papa gave it to me because I love to sew," Caroline explained. "I'm going to turn ten in three weeks, and I'm making a new dress for my birthday." She opened the worktable and pulled out several pieces of lovely blue cloth.

"I like the color," Rhonda said.

"It reminds me of Lake Ontario on a sunny day," Caroline told her. "If we could still shop in Kingston, I'd buy some lace trim."

"My mother is teaching me to make lace with

thread and a little shuttle," Rhonda said.

Rhonda knew how to *make* lace? "I've never seen anyone do that," Caroline admitted. "But I do like to embroider." She proudly pulled her current project from her apron pocket. "My papa loves Lake Ontario, and I've been stitching a map of the lakeshore for him."

"But . . . whatever will he do with it?" Rhonda asked.

Something about the way Rhonda asked the question made Caroline wish she'd just put the embroidery away in the worktable instead of showing it off. "One of the carpenters at my family's shipyard has promised to frame my embroidery as a fire screen," she explained. Caroline didn't tell Rhonda that she loved to imagine Papa relaxing by the hearth in the evenings, shielded from the fire's heat by the screen.

Rhonda's gaze wandered from the embroidery. "What's that?" she asked, pointing at a short length of knotted rope inside the worktable.

Caroline stroked the knots with one finger. "The British are holding my papa prisoner in Kingston because he's a shipbuilder. He was teaching me how to tie different knots. We were working on this together while we were out sailing the day he was captured."

"Oh, I see." Rhonda's mouth closed in a very tight line. She turned away as if she weren't interested.

Our life must seem boring to someone who comes from a big city like Albany and who knows how to make lace, Caroline thought. She tucked her treasures back into the worktable and closed the lid. "Grandmother likely has the tea ready," she said. "Let's go down to the kitchen."

The next morning, Mama woke Caroline before dawn. "The sky is cloudy, but there's no sign of storms," Mama said. "We'll sail today. Grandmother is cooking breakfast."

Caroline quickly dressed and hurried downstairs. Soon she would be in Upper Canada, where Papa was! Upper Canada, where enemy soldiers and sailors were headquartered. By the time Caroline sat down to crisp bacon, biscuits warm from the oven, and a bowl of steaming oatmeal, her stomach seemed to be tying itself into knots that any sailor would envy.

The Hathaways filed into the kitchen as Caroline was struggling to finish her meal. "Please, sit down," Caroline said. "I'll fetch more bowls."

She was reaching for the ladle in the oatmeal pot when an odd knock sounded on the front door. *Knock . . . knock-knock. Knock . . . knock-knock.*

"Father!" Amelia squealed. She raced from the kitchen. Rhonda's face lit up with joy as she hurried after her sister.

"It's his special knock," Mrs. Hathaway explained. "Please, come—he'll want to meet you."

Grandmother started to rise, but then winced in pain and sank back onto her chair. "The oatmeal will scorch if I don't keep an eye on it," she said. "You two go."

Caroline and Mama found a tall man standing in the hall. He held Amelia on one hip and had his other arm around Rhonda.

Caroline's feet decided to stop walking.

Mama paused, bending close. "Caroline? Are you well?"

"Yes, fine," she whispered. She didn't want to admit to Mama that the sight of Rhonda and Amelia greeting their father had given her a stab of envy.

After introductions were made, Lieutenant Hathaway bowed to Mama and Caroline. "Thank you for sheltering my family," he said. "With your permission, I will visit often. But now I must return to my duties."

"You may come any time," Mama assured him. "Caroline, why don't we go pack and let the Hathaways say their good-byes."

Caroline was glad to leave the Hathaways behind. Once upstairs, she set out two heavy wool shawls, her flannel petticoat, and warm gloves. Mama brought her a canvas sack that was coated with wax to keep out water.

"May I take my embroidery?" Caroline asked. "When I'm worried, it helps me to stitch."

"That's a fine idea," Mama said. "I think I shall take my knitting, for much the same reason."

Mrs. Hathaway and Rhonda decided to see the Abbotts off. "We need to get familiar with Sackets Harbor," Mrs. Hathaway said. She and Mama walked ahead of the two girls.

Caroline was so excited and nervous about the trip that she wanted to run straight to the harbor. Still, she tried to make Rhonda feel comfortable. "You can't get lost in the village," Caroline assured her as they turned right onto the main street. "This road leads to the marketplace and the harbor." She pointed ahead.

"It *would* be hard to get lost in such a tiny village," Rhonda remarked.

Caroline felt her cheeks grow hot. She was getting tired of Rhonda Hathaway acting superior! Rhonda might wear fancy clothes, and know how to make lace, and have a papa she could see every single day. But Caroline refused to let Rhonda make her feel ashamed of her home.

Instead, Caroline lifted her chin the way her cousin Lydia did when she wanted to look like a fine lady. "I suppose Sackets Harbor *is* small compared to Albany," Caroline said, her tone chilly as an October lake. "But it's growing fast."

In truth, Caroline hardly recognized her village. Since the war began, the streets had become so crowded! She saw noisy sailors wearing dirty canvas trousers and bright shirts. Stiff-backed marines in blue coats with white crossbelts over their chests marched crisply down the road. And local farmers and clerks who'd joined the militia strode by wearing whatever they pleased.

The frosty morning was filled with commotion. Workmen pounded hammers and manned big saws. Officers bellowed orders. Local farmwives who had set up shop in the marketplace called to passersby. Horses clopped past. Occasionally, Caroline heard the shuddering boom of artillery or the sharp pop of musketry as soldiers practiced.

"Being around soldiers must seem strange to you," Rhonda said coolly. "I'm accustomed to it. This isn't the first time we've traveled with my father's regiment. We like being close to him."

Caroline felt another stab of jealousy. She pointed ahead. "There's *my* papa's shipyard," she said proudly. "He and his men are the best shipbuilders in New York."

Rhonda flushed pink. "Well, *my* father—"

"Come along, girls," Mama called, turning to beckon them forward. Caroline thought that Mama looked nervous and excited, too.

Mr. Tate hurried to meet them. "Good morning," he said, eyeing the bags Caroline and Mama carried. "Today's the day, eh?"

He already understands where we're going, Caroline

thought. She smiled gratefully at Mr. Tate. She knew that Mama dared leave the shipyard only because she trusted him to handle things.

Mama introduced the Hathaways and then said, "Mr. Tate, I need to speak with you in the office about what must be done here in the next few days."

"I'll be right along, ma'am," Mr. Tate said. He was a big man, and weathered from his years as a sailor. His straw hat had been caked with tar to shed rain. His corduroy jacket was well worn. Mr. Tate didn't care about fancy clothes, but he knew more about shaping wood into ships than just about anyone.

"I wish you good luck on your journey, Miss Caroline," Mr. Tate said.

"Thank you," Caroline said. Then she leaned close and whispered, "I'm so excited I might burst! I don't know if I should feel hopeful or worried."

"If anyone can convince the British to release your father, it's Mrs. Abbott," he told Caroline. "So all you need to worry about is getting home in time for your birthday." His eyes twinkled. "I hear there's a special dinner planned. Mrs. Abbott was kind enough to invite me."

"I'm trying to decide whether to ask Grandmother for an apple pie or a burnt-sugar cake," Caroline told him.

Mr. Tate grinned. "Fine eating either way. And I have a special gift in mind for my favorite young lady."

"Thank you, Mr. Tate." Caroline gave him a warm smile.

Mr. Tate hurried to the office. Mrs. Hathaway left the girls and wandered away to look over the yard. Caroline turned her attention to the gunboat the men were building. It was a heavy ship with a flat bottom, perfect for traveling through the shallow waters along Lake Ontario's shore and in the Saint Lawrence River nearby.

Caroline had many different feelings when she visited the shipyard these days. She missed Papa's quiet presence terribly, but she was also proud of Mama and the workers. "That gunboat will carry troops and equipment, and maybe go into battle, too," she explained to Rhonda. "Mr. Tate and the workers have done a wonderful job."

"I heard Mr. Tate say he's coming to your birthday

dinner," Rhonda murmured. "He must know your family very well."

Caroline turned around. "Mr. Tate started working for Papa before I was born. He looks out for Mama and me."

"How nice that you have someone to take your father's place," Rhonda said.

For a moment, Caroline could hardly breathe. "Why—no, it's not like that at all!" she stammered. As if someone, *anyone*, could take Papa's place at the shipyard or in her heart! It was a terrible thing to suggest.

Rhonda tugged one of her mittens up over her wrist. "All I meant was that it must be nice to have someone like—"

"*Nothing* is nice right now!" Caroline cried. "You don't know what it's like to have your father gone."

"I do know," Rhonda retorted. "My father's been in the army my whole life. If we didn't follow him every time he was posted somewhere new, I'd probably never see him!"

"It's *not* the same," Caroline insisted. Suddenly all of her worry and envy and nervousness turned into anger. "I wish you *hadn't* followed your papa this time. I wish you'd stayed in Albany!"

Rhonda's eyes narrowed. Then she turned her back on Caroline and walked away.

I shouldn't have spoken so, Caroline thought. Her words had been truthful, but also unkind.

Before she could decide what to do, Mama stepped from the office. "Caroline?" she called. "Let's get started."

As Mama and Caroline settled into the skiff, Caroline tried to put the argument with Rhonda out of her mind. They were off to find Papa. Nothing was more important than that.

On Enemy Ground

ama began to row the skiff through the harbor. Several honking geese flew past. Caroline heard sailors on a nearby schooner bellowing "Heave, heave, heave!" as they raised a sail. Perhaps they would head out to search for British ships. *And we're heading out on a dangerous trip, too,* Caroline thought.

Once they reached the open lake Mama paused, shrugging her shoulders to ease her muscles. "The wind is perfect today," she said.

Caroline lifted her face and tried to consider the wind against her cheeks as Papa had taught her. "The breeze seems strong, but not *too* strong," she agreed. "Shall we set the sail?"

As Caroline raised the sail, her spirits lifted, too. She hadn't traveled on Lake Ontario in all the months since the British had captured Papa. In spite of her worries, being back on the water made her happy. She closed her eyes for a moment, feeling the skiff bob on the choppy water. *Papa will come home*, Caroline told herself. She'd prove herself steady enough to make a good captain. And one day Papa would build a sloop just for her.

The skiff rose on a little wave and then dropped again. Caroline's eyes flew open as an icy spray of water hit her face.

"Try not to get splashed," Mama warned. Her cheeks were already bright red from cold.

Caroline wiped her cheek with one hand. The wind that filled their sail also knifed through her cloak. This was a dangerous time of year to travel in such a small boat. If a storm blew up and swamped the little skiff, she and Mama might freeze before reaching shore or getting rescued.

"I'll stay dry," Caroline promised. "Knowing that Papa built this skiff makes me feel safe. It's almost as if he's here, taking care of us. And maybe Papa will soon be sailing it himself!"

Mama smiled. "That's a lovely thought."

As they settled in for the long journey, Caroline found her mind bouncing between thoughts of Papa and thoughts of the quarrel she'd had with Rhonda that morning. *You can mend things with Rhonda when you get home,* Caroline told herself. Still, Rhonda's comments echoed in her mind.

"Mama," Caroline said finally, "Mr. Tate said you'd invited him to my birthday dinner."

"I did," Mama said. "I want the evening to be special."

Caroline heard Rhonda's voice again: *How nice that you have someone to take your father's place.* "All I want is Papa home for my birthday," Caroline said.

Mama's face softened. "We both want that, and I pray that he will be. But even if he isn't, we'll have a real party. Now that the Hathaways have come, there will be lots of people to celebrate your birthday."

Caroline looked out over the restless water. "I think . . . that is, I'd rather have just family at my birthday dinner."

"I see," Mama said slowly. "Don't you like Rhonda? I thought it would be nice for you to have another girl in the house."

"I don't want another girl in the house," Caroline grumbled. She felt tears threaten and blinked hard to hold them back. "And Mr. Tate can never take Papa's place!"

Mama looked startled. "Of *course* not! But today, let's think just about getting Papa home, shall we?"

Caroline's cheeks grew hot with embarrassment. She was determined to be helpful on this trip. Fretting about her quarrel with Rhonda wouldn't help anything.

"Yes," she agreed firmly. "Let's think just about getting Papa home."

The trip took all day. Mama sailed close to shore as they traveled, threading their way around islands. She landed the skiff several times on deserted beaches so that she and Caroline could stretch their legs, rub their arms for warmth, and snack on bread and apples.

Caroline felt that knotted feeling in her stomach again as they reached the north shore of the Saint Lawrence River. That mighty river marked the border between New York and Upper Canada. *We're in enemy territory now,* she thought. She didn't see any British ships, but she knew they must be patrolling nearby.

As Caroline watched the wooded shoreline of Upper Canada glide by, she imagined Papa slipping away from his guards and hiding in the forest. Sometimes she and Mama sailed past Indian camps or little clearings where settlers had built log homes. The shelters and cabins looked no different from those Caroline knew in New York. It seemed so strange to think that the people who lived in them were likely loyal to the British!

Finally Mama said, "We're getting close to Uncle Aaron and Aunt Martha's farm. You've done well today, Caroline."

Mama's praise made Caroline feel good, and she was glad she hadn't complained about the cold or her growing hunger. Still, by the time the cabin came into view a few miles east of Kingston, Caroline felt hollow and frozen to the bone. Her arms ached from helping with the oars. She used her last bit of strength to help Mama pull the skiff up on the shore.

Lydia and Oliver's parents had moved their family to Upper Canada a few years before the war began, when the border between the two countries hardly seemed to matter at all. Caroline knew they'd worked hard to build their small cabin and clear a few acres to farm.

Twilight was falling as Caroline and Mama hurried into the yard. "It seems very quiet," Mama murmured.

Caroline looked around. The clearing seemed deserted. *Oh no*, she thought with dismay. *What will we do if no one is home?*

Mama strode to the front door and knocked. A curtain over the front window twitched, as if someone was peeping out.

Mama knocked again. "Aaron?" she called. "It's your sister!"

The door finally opened, and Uncle Aaron appeared. Caroline had never been so glad to see her uncle!

"Come inside, quickly," he said. His tone was hushed, and his gaze darted nervously about the empty farmyard.

Caroline followed him and Mama into the cabin. Lydia hurried forward and crushed Caroline into a hug.

"We've got news," Mama said. "Oliver is free! He arrived at our house yesterday."

Aunt Martha caught her breath, and her eyes filled with tears. Uncle Aaron whispered, "God be praised." Lydia squeezed Caroline's hand.

Then Uncle Aaron cleared his throat. "It's wonderful to see you both, and we want to hear more. But first—did you sail over?"

"Our skiff is down on the beach," Caroline said.

"We'll have to hide it," Uncle Aaron said. "Martha, Lydia, come help with the boat. Caroline, you stay here and warm up."

Lydia followed her parents and Mama outside. Alone in the cabin, Caroline shivered with fear as much as cold. Why was Uncle Aaron acting so strange? And why was he so worried about the skiff?

She sank onto a stool by the big hearth and stared at the crackling flames. A kettle of stew bubbled over the fire. The room smelled of cider vinegar, hickory smoke, venison, and molasses pie. Caroline breathed in the comforting harvesttime scents.

When her fingers were warm enough, she tugged off her gloves, reached into her travel bag, and pulled out her embroidery. *I'm glad I brought this*, she thought, even though she had to lean toward the fire to see well enough to stitch. She smoothed the embroidery over her lap and studied it, thinking of the colors Lake Ontario showed on sunny days. She decided to add streaks of green to the blue water she'd already created with silk thread. The familiar challenge of blending colors occupied her thoughts and calmed her hands.

By the time the others returned, Caroline's shivering had stopped. "We're glad you're here," Aunt Martha said. She kissed Caroline's cheek. "We'll dish up some stew. You'll feel better after a hot meal."

Caroline tucked her embroidery away. Uncle Aaron sat down on the far side of the hearth and gestured Mama into another chair. "I'm sorry if I didn't seem welcoming," he said to Caroline. "These are dangerous times. We've learned to be cautious when we hear voices outside. It might be friends coming, or it might be Loyalists—people who support the British."

Caroline's fingers trembled as she accepted a bowl from Lydia. The stew was thick with tender chunks of venison, potatoes, and carrots. After one bite, Caroline felt a little better.

Uncle Aaron took his clay pipe from its holder near the hearth, filled the bowl with tobacco, and used a long curled wood shaving to light it. "Since the war began, things have become difficult for newcomers like us," he explained. "People who settled here thirty years ago suspect that we are still Americans at heart and not truly loyal to King George. They think we moved north only to gain farmland."

"And they are right," Aunt Martha murmured. She ladled stew into another wooden bowl.

"I wanted to stay out of this war altogether," Uncle Aaron said. "But by law I must serve in the British militia. I could be called to duty any moment."

"Oh no," Caroline whispered. Uncle Aaron might end up fighting his former friends and neighbors! She glanced at Lydia and saw misery in her cousin's face.

Uncle Aaron sighed. "I've examined my heart. I cannot stay here and fight for the king. So Martha and I have decided to move back to New York. We've been building a boat—secretly, in the woods. If our luck holds, we'll finish the boat in time to cross the Saint Lawrence River before it ices over. But if our Loyalist neighbors realize what we're doing, we could be arrested as traitors."

Caroline gasped. Traitors could be imprisoned—
or hanged. She put her bowl down, no longer hungry.

"We believe some of our neighbors are spying on
us already," Lydia added. She crossed her arms over
her chest, clutching her shoulders as if she were cold.

Now Caroline understood why Uncle Aaron had
wanted to hide the skiff. If the Loyalists saw it, they
might think he was planning to use it to escape back
to New York. "Please be careful," she begged.

"We will," Uncle Aaron promised. But even in
the flickering firelight, worry showed on his face.

Caroline's stomach clenched tighter. Would
Uncle Aaron's family manage to set sail before harsh
weather—or a Loyalist neighbor—prevented them
from leaving?

Uncle Aaron turned to Mama. "Please tell us about
Oliver—is he well?"

Mama and Caroline told the story of Oliver's release.
"He's worn down, but he'll be fine," Mama finished.

"He brought bad news, though," Caroline said. "He
told us that the British are planning to send prisoners
to Halifax. Oliver thinks that if Papa ends up on a ship
to Halifax, he should try to escape."

"That's why we're here," Mama said. "I'm going to argue for my husband's release. If I fail, I'll try to let him know what Oliver advises."

Uncle Aaron got to his feet and began to pace the room. "But if John does escape, what then? The weather is already harsh, and it will only get colder. How would he get back to New York?"

"Papa could do it!" Caroline insisted. Her aunt glanced nervously toward the door, and Caroline lowered her voice. "He knows this end of the lake as well as anybody—"

"That won't keep him safe," Uncle Aaron broke in. "Yes, he knows the marshes and the currents. And at one time, he knew everyone who lived along these shores. But that's no longer enough."

Aunt Martha explained, "Your father has no way of knowing which families he can trust, or where the British gunboats patrol. If the British were to capture him a second time, he would be treated much more harshly."

"Then we must get him the information he needs," Mama said briskly. "Perhaps I can tuck a note between the pages of the Bible I brought, or hide it away in some food. Surely the British won't stop a worried wife from bringing her husband a Bible and a cake!"

"If you're allowed to visit him at all," Uncle Aaron said grimly, "whatever you carry will be searched. And if you're caught with such a note, you'll be arrested."

Lydia slipped her hand into Caroline's. "I wish we were *all* safe in Sackets Harbor," she whispered.

Caroline wished the skiff were big enough to carry everyone back to New York. She wished she could cuddle Inkpot's rumbling warmth against her cheek. She wished she were as brave as her grandmother.

Oh, Grandmother, she thought, *everything is even worse than we feared.*

And there in the little cabin in enemy territory, miles from home and safety, Caroline fancied she could hear Grandmother's answer: *It is, eh? Well, what are you going to do about it? Come now, girl. You're not giving up, are you?*

I don't want to give up, Caroline protested silently. But how could *she* help get Papa the information he needed?

This time, Grandmother didn't answer.

Caroline reached for her embroidery and ran a

finger over the map she'd stitched so carefully. *We're right here,* she thought, touching the spot where Lydia's cabin stood. Then she ran her finger over the smooth stitches that formed the nearby shoreline. *If Papa is able to escape, he'll need to follow this route to safety . . .*

"Oh!" she said suddenly. "I have an idea!"

Papa

After an early breakfast the next morning, Mama and Caroline sailed on to Kingston. Caroline was excited and nervous and tired. She had sat up late the night before, working carefully on her embroidered map. Uncle Aaron and Aunt Martha had identified the location of every old friend who could no longer be trusted, as well as waterways patrolled most often by British gunboats. Caroline had carefully stitched a warning X at each trouble spot.

Now her heart seemed to bang against her ribs as they approached Point Frederick, where Papa was being held. She hadn't been so close to Papa in months. She had to clench her teeth to keep from yelling, *Mama and I are here, Papa! We've come to help you escape!*

As she and Mama pulled the skiff up on the beach,

a young soldier trotted toward them. He wore white trousers and a scarlet coat with a white crossbelt. His musket held a long bayonet. His black-and-gold hat was so tall that he looked especially threatening.

"Mama," Caroline whispered. Her knees felt wobbly.

Mama squeezed Caroline's shoulder. "Have courage, Caroline. If we are not able to win Papa's release, his best chance of escape depends on you and your map."

The soldier reached them. "Madam," he began, "this is a military area."

"I understand that, sir," Mama said. "But my husband is being held here unjustly. I came to see whoever is in charge."

"That's Major Humphries," he said stiffly. "Follow me."

The soldier led them into the fort area. *In truth,* Caroline thought, *there is not much here!* She saw only a single two-story blockhouse. Hammers banged as soldiers labored to build a rough wall around the grounds. A civilian man was yelling at an ox pulling a wagon piled with lumber.

She stumbled over a rut left by wagon wheels, but she couldn't tear her gaze from the buildings. Papa was *here*! Was he in that building? Or that other one, over there? Was he watching them through one of the windows? She trembled with the longing to run and search, calling for him.

Mama took Caroline's hand and gave her a warning look: *I know it's difficult to stay calm. But we must not do anything to anger the soldiers.*

The soldier took them to one of the wooden buildings and explained his errand to another sentry. Finally Mama and Caroline were led into a large room that was surprisingly well furnished. A tall chest of drawers gleamed with polish. A mirror hung on one wall, and silver candlesticks and crystal goblets sparkled on a side table.

A stern, gray-haired man with red cheeks sat at a table. He was eating beans and bacon from a china plate. A cup of tea steamed beside it. Several papers were fanned on the table in front of the man's breakfast.

He wiped his mouth on a linen handkerchief and rose to meet Mama and Caroline. "I'm Major Humphries. You're looking for one of the prisoners,

I'm told." He waved his hand toward two chairs. "Please, sit."

Mama introduced them. Caroline perched on the edge of her chair. It seemed impossible that they were truly here, inside a British fort, talking to a British officer!

"You've been holding my husband, John Abbott, since last June," Mama began. "He was taken from a merchant ship before we knew that war had been declared. His absence makes life very difficult for me and my daughter."

Caroline tried to look frightened and needy. That part wasn't hard.

"So I ask you, sir, to release my husband," Mama finished. "He's done nothing wrong."

The major shook his head. "I'm sorry, madam. We know Mr. Abbott is a shipbuilder. We simply cannot release him."

Mama sat very tall, her hands clenched in her lap. For a moment she pressed her lips together. Finally she said, "Well then, sir, I would like to see my husband."

He shook his head. "Can't be done."

"Sir," Mama said sharply, "surely you will not be

so unkind! I have brought a bit of food, a Bible, and a warm shirt. My husband was taken in springtime, and now winter is on its way."

A burst of laughter rang from one of the next rooms. Caroline felt anger rise hot in her chest. How she hated those soldiers and their carefree laughter! She hated Major Humphries and his china plate full of food and his fancy furniture. She hated the British flags hanging on his walls.

Major Humphries rubbed his nose. "This country is full of spies, madam. Just last week a woman selling sweet potatoes tried to smuggle a message to one of the prisoners. No. My answer is no."

Caroline stared at him. She didn't think she could bear to be so close to Papa without being permitted to see him.

"Sir, I *beg* you." Mama's voice trembled. "I have not seen my husband in four months. I—I need to know that he is well."

"I assure you, he is well. And that is the best I can do for you." Major Humphries beckoned to the soldier who had brought them. "Jenner, escort these ladies to their boat. They're going home."

"Please, sir!" Caroline cried desperately. "I haven't seen my papa in ever so long." One tear slid down her cheek, and she didn't wipe it away. "Do you have any daughters?"

Major Humphries studied her. Caroline forced herself to look back at him. The shrill and rattle of a fife and drum drifted into the room.

Finally the officer sighed. "I do, child, I do. They're all grown now, but no less dear to me for that." He looked at Jenner. "Take the child to see her father. A *short* visit, mind! Mrs. Abbott, you may wait in the hall."

Mama took Caroline's hand. "Give Papa my love," she said. The look in her eyes gave Caroline another message: *And give Papa the information he needs to make a safe escape!*

The knots in Caroline's stomach pulled tighter. She was about to see Papa! But she had never imagined visiting him without Mama. *Be brave,* she commanded herself. It was time to stitch together her courage.

Jenner led Caroline across the yard to the blockhouse, where another guard was on duty. He had a long scar on one cheek. Caroline didn't want to think about how he might have gotten that scar.

"The major said she could see Mr. Abbott," Jenner explained to the blockhouse guard. "We need to search her cloak and her basket."

Caroline's skin felt prickly—so much depended on the next few minutes! She placed her basket on a small table by the door. Then she unfastened her cloak and handed it to the guard.

The guard checked the seams and lining to see if she'd hidden anything between the layers of cloth. Jenner poked through Caroline's basket. He turned the wool shirt inside out. He flipped through the small Bible, holding it upside down to make sure no slips of paper had been tucked between the pages. He inspected the bag of apples and dried cherries.

Then the guard pulled out the ginger cakes that Grandmother had sent along and crumbled them in his fingers. "Sorry," he muttered. "Can't be too careful."

The destruction made Caroline angry, but she only nodded. *The cakes don't matter*, she told herself. As long as the soldiers let her keep her embroidery, they could take whatever else they wished.

"What's this?" Corporal Jenner was staring into the

basket. The only thing left was her embroidered map, folded neatly with the stitches inside.

Caroline's heart thumped so loudly that she was surprised he couldn't hear it. "I—it's just some sewing. I wanted . . . that is, when I'm feeling scared, it helps to keep my hands busy." She hated admitting her fear to these soldiers, but it was the truth.

The guard lifted the cloth, made sure nothing was hidden underneath, and piled everything back into the basket. "All right then."

Caroline blew out her breath. The map was safe!

"Follow me," Jenner commanded. He began clomping up the steps.

Just as Caroline turned to follow him, she heard a low voice, almost a whisper, behind her: "Your father misses you."

Caroline whipped her head around and stared at the guard with the scarred cheek. Had he actually *said* that? His face was expressionless, and he jerked his head toward the stairs.

Caroline hurried after Jenner, up the stairs to a small landing. She found herself facing a closed door. Jenner opened it, calling, "Mr. Abbott? Someone to see—"

"*Papa!*" Caroline had barely even glimpsed him, silhouetted against the window, before she barreled into his arms.

"Caroline?" Papa said hoarsely. "Oh, my own dear Caroline!" He squeezed her so tightly that she could hardly breathe. She squeezed back, breathing in his Papa-scent.

The two of them might have stayed so forever if Jenner hadn't coughed to get their attention. Suddenly Caroline remembered Major Humphries' last order: "A *short* visit, mind!" Reluctantly, she pulled herself from Papa's arms.

The room held a cot with a straw mattress and a small table. The table was littered with scraps of wood. Caroline recognized her father's work in a partially completed model sloop. He'd always enjoyed working with his hands, especially making model ships. Caroline was grateful that the guards had provided him with simple tools and supplies.

"You, sit on the bed," Jenner told Papa. "And you, miss, sit over here." He pointed Caroline to a chair. "You two have ten minutes to talk."

"Caroline, quickly, give me news," Papa said.

"How is everyone at home?"

"We're all well," Caroline said firmly. "Mama is here, but the major wouldn't let her see you. Grandmother has some aches, but she's well too. But . . . how are *you*?" Papa was much thinner than she remembered. His shirt was dirty, with several neatly mended rips. His eyes were the same, though, and his gentle smile.

"I'm well also," he said. "Missing you all terribly, of course. But the guards have been kind. I'm allowed to stroll about outside sometimes. One guard plays a game of chess or dominoes with me every day."

Caroline was glad for those things, but looking at the model sloop made her heart ache. Papa was a sailor at heart! He needed to be out on open water, not caged in a tiny room.

She glanced at Jenner. He leaned against the wall, watching.

I can feel sad for Papa later, she reminded herself. Right now she had important work to do, and not much time to do it.

She forced down a wave of panic and tried to look calm as she began to unpack the basket. "I brought you a few things, Papa."

"Leave them on the table," Jenner ordered.

Caroline carefully placed the shirt, the fruit, the crumbled cakes, and the Bible beside the wood scraps.

"Thank you," Papa said. He looked very happy with the gifts.

Caroline glanced again at Jenner, who stared back. She felt as if a clock were ticking inside her chest. She pulled her sewing from the basket, her fingers slick with sweat. She had trouble grasping the needle she'd left threaded with green silk.

"Please, Caroline, talk to me of home," Papa said urgently.

While Caroline tried to think of a way to give Papa the information he needed, she rambled nervously from one story to the next. She'd put up six crocks of pickles, but the bean crop had been poor. Grandmother was still helping her learn to bake bread. Inkpot's latest game involved dropping dead mice by her bed.

And all the while, time raced past.

"Just a few more minutes," Jenner warned.

I have to try! Caroline thought desperately. She might never have another chance. *Papa* might never have another chance.

Just then, men started shouting somewhere outside. "What in heaven's name?" Jenner muttered. He stepped to the window.

Now! Caroline thought. She forced herself to go on with her story. ". . . and Mrs. Shaw set a pan of new soap out to dry in the sun . . ."

As Caroline spoke, she quickly spread her embroidery against the side of her leg, holding it so that Papa could see the map. It showed the eastern tip of Lake Ontario, which she'd created carefully from silk thread. With one shaking finger, Caroline pointed at the new black X she'd stitched on the island where the Baxter family lived—an X to signal *Don't go here. It's not safe.*

Papa glanced at the map and then back at her. He looked puzzled. Caroline met his gaze fiercely, willing him to understand what she was trying to tell him. ". . . and the next time Mrs. Shaw looked out her window," she continued, "she saw a raccoon nibbling at that soap."

Caroline dared a glance at Jenner, who was still watching some commotion in the yard below. Then she moved her finger to another X.

Papa looked completely baffled.

Oh, Papa, please understand! Caroline begged silently. Moving only her finger, she pointed straight at Papa. Then she touched the X and shook her head slightly. *Not—safe!* She mouthed the words silently.

"Blasted oxen are nothing but trouble," Jenner mumbled as he turned away from the window.

Oh no! Caroline thought. She hadn't had a chance to point out every X! Did Papa even understand? She needed more time.

She bent her head and pretended to stitch on one edge of the fabric, leaving the embroidery draped casually over her lap so that Papa could see it. What would happen if Jenner spotted her trick? Would he arrest *her*? Would he punish Papa?

Her voice sounded breathless as she tried to continue her story. "So—so now Seth jokes that we've got the cleanest raccoons in New York."

She darted a glance at Papa. He was studying the map intensely now. "And then—"

"That's all," Jenner said. "Time for you to go."

Caroline's heart felt ready to crack in two.

"Oh, my dear daughter," Papa whispered.

Without asking for permission from Jenner, Caroline ran to her father and gave him another hug. "I'm trying to stay steady," she whispered. "I'm trying to ride the storms through to better weather."

Papa held her close for a moment before gently pulling away. "That's my girl," he said. He swiped at his eyes and then gave her a firm look. "Thank you for coming, Caroline. Thank you for the shirt and the fruit and the Bible." He let his gaze flick to the embroidered map as she folded it back into her basket. "Thank you for *everything*."

Happy Birthday, Caroline

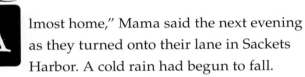

≥ CHAPTER 11 ≥

lmost home," Mama said the next evening as they turned onto their lane in Sackets Harbor. A cold rain had begun to fall. Caroline couldn't remember being so tired. When their house came into view, though, she saw that Grandmother had put a candle in the window. The tiny glow made her feel warm and safe.

"Let's go in the back door," Mama suggested. "Grandmother is likely in the kitchen."

Caroline heard raised voices and laughter as she and Mama walked around the house. *The Hathaways must be in the kitchen with Grandmother,* Caroline thought. She was glad that Grandmother had not been alone while she and Mama were gone. When she remembered saying that she wished Rhonda hadn't followed her father to Sackets Harbor, her face felt hot. She didn't like what Rhonda had said to her about Mr. Tate taking Papa's place. Still, Caroline knew she owed Rhonda an apology.

The kitchen smelled richly of fish and cabbage and spiced cider. Grandmother was sitting by the fire, knitting. And seated at the table were Mrs. Hathaway, the two girls—and their father. Caroline forgot all about her apology.

Lieutenant Hathaway jumped to his feet. "Why, it's Mrs. Abbott and Miss Caroline!"

The room grew noisy with greetings, but Caroline couldn't join in. After having to leave Papa in Upper Canada, seeing Lieutenant Hathaway sitting with *his* family made her hands curl into fists. Papa was the one who should be sitting in this warm kitchen drinking cider!

"I'm happy you're home," Grandmother said, "but sorry to see that you came without John."

Mama shook her head. "The British would not release him."

Mrs. Hathaway took their damp cloaks and hung them up to dry. Grandmother poured cups of hot cider. Amelia carefully passed them around.

Rhonda was the only person who hadn't stood. "I—I'm sorry you weren't able to win your father's freedom," she said to Caroline.

"Oh, my papa will be home soon," Caroline said. Her voice came out louder than she had planned. "*I* showed him the information he needs to escape!"

After a startled silence, Mama said, "Well, we *hope* he will be home soon."

Rhonda's hand was moving beneath the table. Caroline leaned closer to see what she was doing. Why . . . Rhonda was petting Inkpot, who was curled up on her lap!

That was just too much to bear. Caroline ran from the kitchen, pounded up the stairs, and threw herself onto her bed. She was crying into her pillow when she heard footsteps enter the room a few minutes later. Mama sat on the bed beside her.

"It's not *fair*," Caroline said through tears. "This is our house, and *my* papa should be here. And—and while we were away, Rhonda stole Inkpot!"

Mama stroked Caroline's hair. "I'm sure Rhonda did not set out to steal Inkpot, Caroline."

Caroline sniffled miserably.

"Have you thought about how Inkpot felt to have you gone?" Mama asked. "He was probably lonely without you. And Rhonda is probably lonely, too. She's new here in Sackets Harbor, remember."

"I know," Caroline grumbled.

"You were strong and brave on our trip to Upper Canada," Mama said. "We're safe at home now, but I still need you to be strong."

Caroline wiped her eyes. "I'll do better when Papa comes home," she promised.

Mama looked out the window for a long moment. Then she said, "Caroline, we both must accept the fact that Papa may still be gone for a long time. We've done all we can do to help him. Now we must do our best to get along without him."

Caroline whispered, "I—I just wish Lieutenant Hathaway wouldn't visit anymore." It hurt her heart to see someone else's father in the kitchen.

"I know it's hard," Mama said. "But you're almost ten now. You're growing into a young woman. I hope you'll find the courage to be a friend to Rhonda." Mama kissed Caroline's forehead. Then she left her alone.

I'll apologize to Rhonda after Papa comes home, Caroline

thought stubbornly. It would be easier to forgive Rhonda's rude comments when Papa was sitting in his own kitchen. In the meantime, though, she would obey Mama and try to be more friendly.

Caroline didn't feel ready to go downstairs. Instead she went to the sewing box Papa had given her and pulled out a piece of the blue cloth she was using to sew her new dress. She was determined to finish it in time for her birthday. She still wished she could make it fancy with lace, but the color was beautiful.

Surely Papa will come in time for my birthday dinner, she thought. She wanted to wear her new dress. She wanted him to see that she was, as Mama had said, becoming a young lady.

Caroline jumped as something pushed against her leg. "Inkpot!" she cried. She put the blue cloth away and scooped the black cat into her arms. He stopped purring long enough to rub his head against her chin.

Caroline settled back on the bed. "We'll *both* be glad to see Papa come home," she murmured. "He'll be here soon now, I think. Very soon."

The next morning, Caroline waited until she saw
Rhonda slip outside to fetch water. Caroline grabbed
her own shawl and hurried after her. The rain had
stopped, but gloomy clouds still hung low in the sky.

She joined Rhonda at the well. "I . . . that is, would
you like some help?" Caroline asked politely.

"That would be nice," Rhonda said, just as politely.

The girls worked together to fill two buckets. Then
they stood, as if neither one knew what to say. A crow
landed on the fence to inspect what was left of the
garden. Finally Caroline said, "Let's take these buckets
into the kitchen."

For the rest of that day, Caroline and Rhonda didn't
argue. They both helped Grandmother with chores
and never got cross with each other. But they didn't
laugh together or share stories. Caroline thought the
icy politeness felt almost as bad as arguing did.

As the days passed, Caroline wished that she knew
how to make friends with Rhonda. Oliver had joined
the navy, so he wasn't at the house very often. Seth still
spent most of his time traveling and delivering mail.
Inkpot was a comfort. Grandmother kept Caroline
busy. But Caroline still felt hollow inside.

Every day, she watched for her father. When she visited the shipyard, she walked down to the dock, searching the harbor in case he'd escaped and found a canoe or gotten a ride on someone's boat. At home, she watched the lane for a tired traveler. *Everything will be better when Papa gets home*, Caroline thought over and over.

One week crawled by. Then another. Uncle Aaron, Aunt Martha, and Lydia arrived safely from Upper Canada, and Caroline, Mama, and Grandmother welcomed them joyfully into the Abbotts' house for the winter.

Two days later, Caroline's birthday arrived, frosty and clear. But Papa had not come home.

Caroline had just wriggled into her new blue dress that afternoon when Rhonda knocked on the bedroom door. She looked uncertain. Caroline felt uncertain, too. And very, very sad.

"Excuse me," Rhonda said. She met Caroline's gaze and then quickly looked away. "If you wish, I'd be glad to arrange your hair for you."

"Like yours?" Caroline asked. Rhonda's hairstyle *did* make her look grown-up. "All right."

Rhonda stood behind Caroline and picked up the hairbrush. "Your new dress is pretty."

"It's not as fine as yours," Caroline said with a little shrug.

Rhonda sighed. "Mama says we have to wear nice clothes because Papa is an officer. I wish I didn't have to worry about getting my dress dirty all the time. You're lucky—you have a nice dress *and* one that's easy to work in."

Caroline blinked in surprise. She'd never thought about it that way. She couldn't see Rhonda's face, which made it easier for her to say, "I'm sorry we quarreled that morning in the shipyard."

"I am, too," Rhonda said quickly. "I didn't mean to hurt your feelings."

"And I didn't mean to hurt yours," Caroline said. "I just miss my papa so *much*."

Rhonda took several brushstrokes before saying, "It sounds as if you spent a lot of time together before he was captured."

"My papa and I both love sailing on Lake Ontario

better than anything else in the world," Caroline said.
"Sometimes I went to the shipyard with him, too."

Rhonda began twisting Caroline's hair into a knot.
"My father loves being in the army best," she said.
"Mother and Amelia and I follow him from place
to place." She picked up a hairpin. "I think . . . well,
I think I felt jealous of you. Knowing that you and your
father were sailing together before he was captured
made me envious. My father never does anything like
that with me."

Rhonda was envious of *her*? Caroline thought
about that.

"And if something happened to my father," Rhonda
added, "I don't think any of his army friends would
look out for us the way Mr. Tate looks after you and
your mother."

"Oh," Caroline said in a small voice.

"There," Rhonda said. "I'm finished."

Caroline picked up the small hand mirror on
her dresser and caught her breath. She looked so
grown-up! "Why, I almost don't recognize myself—
but it's pretty. I look like a young lady. Thank you,
Rhonda."

"You're welcome." Rhonda smiled. "It sounds as if everyone is gathering. Shall we go downstairs?"

For the first time in months, Mama had set the table in the dining room. Caroline hesitated in the doorway. She'd been dreading this moment. If Papa came home right this minute and found a party under way, would he think she'd forgotten him? For a few seconds, Caroline felt frozen.

Then she looked at her family and friends gathered around the table. Uncle Aaron, Aunt Martha, Lydia, and Oliver looked happier than Caroline could remember. Mr. Tate had worn his best clothes. The Hathaways' pretty dresses were like an indoor rainbow of blue, green, and yellow. Seth didn't have a fine shirt to change into, but he'd clearly scrubbed up as best he could. His hair was combed away from his face, and his grin came from the heart.

All these people want to help celebrate my birthday, Caroline thought. A warm feeling slowly filled the frozen place inside.

When everyone was seated, one chair remained

empty. "Mama?" Caroline asked. "Is someone else coming?"

"I thought we'd leave an extra chair," Mama said. "Whenever Papa does come home, it will be waiting."

"I like that idea," Caroline said. "I like it very much."

Mama and Grandmother had prepared a feast: stuffed whitefish, lima beans, cabbage and apples, carrot pudding, and *two* desserts—an apple pie and a burnt-sugar cake.

After the plates had been cleared away, Caroline received several gifts. Grandmother gave her a tin biscuit cutter. Mama gave her a tiny pair of sharp scissors, perfect for snipping embroidery thread.

"And this is from me," Rhonda said. She passed Caroline a handkerchief folded around something small and delicate.

"Oh!" Caroline said, feeling surprised. She hadn't expected a gift from Rhonda. Caroline opened the handkerchief and held up a long piece of lace. "It's so pretty!"

"I made it myself," Rhonda told her shyly. "It's not nearly as fancy as what you might have purchased in Kingston."

Suddenly, Caroline didn't care a bit about fancy lace from Kingston. "It will be perfect on my new dress," she assured Rhonda. "Just perfect." She studied the delicate loops of white cotton thread. "I can't *imagine* how you made this."

"I could show you," Rhonda offered. "All you do is use the little shuttle to make rows of knots, which form those loops."

"Really?" Caroline's eyes went wide with surprise. "I'm good at tying knots!" She and Rhonda exchanged a smile. A real smile this time.

"Speaking of knots," Mr. Tate began, and then he stopped to clear his throat. "Miss Caroline, I don't have a package to give you," he said. "I thought . . . Well, do you know how to make a French hitch knot?"

Caroline shook her head. "No."

He beamed. "Well, young miss, I'm going to teach you. Once you've learned that knot, I'll help you make the prettiest cider-jug cover you ever saw. Since the jug in your papa's office isn't covered, it could easily get nicked or broken. We'll make a nice cover, and he'll see it as soon as he returns."

Caroline jumped up so fast, her chair almost fell

over. She ran around the table and hugged Mr. Tate. "What a wonderful gift," she said. "Thank you."

Caroline thought that was the last present, but after she'd settled back in her place, Aunt Martha came around the table and handed her a parcel. "This isn't really from us," she said, exchanging a glance with Uncle Aaron and Lydia. "We're just delivering it."

Puzzled, Caroline pulled away the cloth wrapping and found a wooden box. The lid was decorated with tiny bits of golden straw that had been pasted into fancy designs around the edge. Darker pieces of straw spelled out *CAROLINE*.

"I can keep my embroidery silks in here," Caroline said, turning the delicate box in her hands. "But . . . who made it?"

Aunt Martha smiled. "All we know for *certain* is that it was waiting on our doorstep one morning, right before we left Upper Canada."

Caroline gasped. "It's from Papa!" She remembered seeing scraps of wood in his room at Point Frederick, and his mattress had been stuffed with straw. "But how did he get it to you?"

Uncle Aaron spread his hands. "We don't know!

There was no note. Putting anything in writing was likely too dangerous. But we think one of the guards at the fort brought it to us as a favor to your father."

Caroline gently touched the box with one finger. Her heart had been filled with anger and hatred toward the British. It was hard to take in this new idea, that one of them had done such a kindness. She suddenly remembered the guard with the scar on his cheek who had whispered after her on the stairs, *Your father misses you.*

Tears filled Caroline's eyes. One spilled down her cheek before she could wipe it away. "Excuse me," she said, pushing back her chair. She hurried into the kitchen, scooped Inkpot from the rug by the hearth, and held him close. He began to purr.

Grandmother followed her into the room, leaning heavily on her cane. "Caroline? What's wrong?"

"Everyone has been so kind to me," Caroline began. "Even a British soldier!"

Grandmother raised her eyebrows, waiting for Caroline to continue.

"It doesn't seem fair to Papa to feel happy and

to celebrate . . ." Caroline's voice trailed away. It was hard to explain her tangled feelings.

Grandmother regarded her. "What do you think your papa would say if he were here?"

"Well," Caroline said slowly, "I don't think he'd want me to be unhappy."

"I *know* he wouldn't," Grandmother said firmly. "You're holding him in your heart, Caroline. That's what matters."

Caroline considered that idea, studying it like a new color of silk to be stitched into a picture. "I think you're right," she admitted finally. "But Grandmother? I'll never stop hoping. Never stop waiting for Papa to come home."

"Of course not," Grandmother said. "None of us will."

Caroline heard the murmur of conversation from the next room, where people she loved had gathered to honor her birthday. She reached for her grandmother's hand. "Come along," she said. "Let's go back to the party."

Winter Wishes

CHAPTER 12

December 1812

W inter blew into Sackets Harbor soon after Caroline's birthday. For weeks now, the little village had had nothing but bitter cold, blinding blizzards, and howling winds. There had been no word from Papa. Caroline held him in her heart and waited, trying to stay steady.

Cousin Lydia's family had settled into the Abbotts' home along with the Hathaways. The Livingstons planned to stay until spring, when they could make a fresh start on a farm in New York. Caroline's crowded house bustled with activity as Christmas approached.

This morning, icy winds shook the windowpanes of the bedchamber that Caroline now shared with Lydia and Rhonda, and the spicy smell of gingerbread floated up from the kitchen. The three girls sat close together on Caroline's bed, inspecting a colorful pile of fabric scraps. They were making a doll to give to Rhonda's little sister for Christmas.

The gift was Caroline's idea, and she felt proud that Lydia and Rhonda were excited about it. She wanted this project to go well!

Caroline held up two pieces of cloth. "Shall we use this brown cotton for the doll's dress?" she asked. "Or the blue silk?"

Lydia pointed at the blue fabric. "Let's use that beautiful silk!"

"I don't know if that's wise," said Rhonda. "Amelia doesn't always take care of things as well as she should. Perhaps the brown fabric would be better. It's sturdier, and it won't show dirt."

"What do you think, Caroline?" Lydia asked.

Caroline was pleased by the question. The older girls didn't always ask her opinion. "If we give Amelia a doll wearing a pretty party dress," she said, "I think she'll take good care of it."

Rhonda tipped her head thoughtfully. "You may be right. Yes. Let's use the blue silk."

Without warning, the door opened and Amelia, who was four years old, peeked inside. Her face brightened when she saw the older girls. "What are you doing?" she asked as Lydia quickly hid the doll behind her back.

"Amelia!" Rhonda scolded. "You mustn't enter a room without knocking. Go away."

Amelia's smile faded. "Why can't I come in?" she asked. Her face puckered as if she was about to cry.

Caroline jumped up and led Amelia back into the hall. She couldn't tell Amelia that she'd almost ruined her own Christmas surprise! "We—we're busy with something, that's all."

"Everyone's always busy." Amelia thrust out her lower lip in a pout. "I just want someone to play with me!"

I wish Amelia had children near her own age to play with, Caroline thought. She crouched down so that she could look Amelia in the eye. "I'm sorry, but we can't start any games now. Rhonda and Lydia and I will leave for lessons soon. Why don't you go ask my grandmother if she needs help in the kitchen?"

Caroline waited until Amelia had plodded downstairs before going back into the bedroom. "She's gone," Caroline reported.

"It will be hard to keep this doll a secret until Christmas!" Rhonda said. "We'd better finish our planning now." She draped the blue cloth around the doll as if imagining the dress. "I'll make some lace trim."

"And I've got an old glove we can cut up to make shoes," Caroline added. "Amelia shall have the prettiest doll in New York State!"

Lydia pulled some white cloth from the pile of scraps. "We'll need to make the doll a petticoat."

"Two petticoats," Rhonda said.

"If it were up to you, we'd make six petticoats," Lydia teased. "You're always cold!"

Rhonda laughed, fingering the scraps. "Caroline, I'm glad you suggested that we make this gift for Amelia. She'll be so pleased."

"I know Amelia wasn't able to bring any toys with her when you moved here," Caroline said sympathetically. Rhonda and Amelia had brought only necessities, because their parents had known it would be difficult to find even a small room to rent in the tiny village where Lieutenant Hathaway was posted after the war began.

"We couldn't bring much with us," Rhonda agreed. She looked at Lydia. "We were able to carry more than your family could, though. I can't imagine having to sneak away from home in the dead of night, as you did!"

"Escaping from Upper Canada *was* scary," Lydia admitted. "But we made it here safely. And as soon as my father finds a new place to farm, we'll start over again." She lifted her chin, as if facing a big challenge she was determined to win. "I'm glad we'll be here for Christmas, though."

"And since Christmas is just a week away," Rhonda reminded them, "we'll need to work quickly to finish this gift."

The reminder that Christmas was approaching made Caroline feel both excited and anxious. She had hemmed new handkerchiefs for her mother, her grandmother, her aunt and uncle, and Mrs. Hathaway. She'd secretly sewn a warm winter muff for Lydia, too. But she still didn't have a Christmas gift for Rhonda! Rhonda already had a muff to warm her hands, and several handkerchiefs with her initials embroidered in silk. Try as she might, Caroline hadn't been able to think of a single good idea for her friend.

Well, at least I had a good idea for Amelia's gift, Caroline thought. She was sure that Amelia would love the doll. And it was great fun to sew the doll and plan her clothes with Rhonda and Lydia. She smiled at the other girls. "I can embroider a face on the doll," she said, "but what shall we use for hair?"

"When my mother knit mittens for Amelia, she had a little yarn left over," Rhonda said. "The yarn isn't dyed, though—it's just white. Do you think we might be able to color it?"

Lydia giggled. "You mustn't ask *Caroline* about dyeing yarn." She nudged Caroline in the ribs. "Remember when we were little, and you decided to dye yarn with pokeberries?"

"You helped," Caroline protested. "It wasn't all my fault."

"What wasn't your fault?" Rhonda asked.

"By the time we were finished, our hands were as purple as the yarn," Caroline confessed.

Lydia flopped down on the bed, laughing. "Our mothers scolded us, but we could tell that they thought it was funny."

Rhonda snickered. "It must have looked as if you both were wearing horrid purple gloves!"

Lydia held her arms in the air gracefully. "My dear Miss Hathaway," she said as if she were a fine lady, "purple gloves are the newest style! All the French ladies are wearing them."

"Oh, my," Rhonda said. "I am sorely behind the times."

Caroline pretended to look down her nose at Rhonda. "We shall show you *all* the latest fashions."

Rhonda got her giggles under control. "Perhaps we shouldn't dye the yarn for Amelia's doll."

"It will be *fine*," Caroline promised. "I'll ask Grandmother to help us this time."

Someone knocked on the door. Caroline thrust the doll beneath her pillow.

Mrs. Hathaway stepped inside. "Gracious!" she said. "I could hear you girls laughing from downstairs. It's almost time for your lessons. Tidy up your sewing, and then you may be off to the shipyard."

There was no school in Sackets Harbor, so Caroline's mother sometimes gave the three girls lessons. Since Mama was busy managing Abbott's Shipyard, the girls gathered in the office there, huddling by the stove in one corner.

"Ready for the last arithmetic problem?" Mama asked.

The girls nodded.

"Listen carefully," Mama said. "A captain loads a ship with a barrel of whale oil that weighs two hundred and sixty pounds, a barrel of salt that weighs ninety-five pounds, and a barrel of fish that weighs one hundred and fourteen pounds. How many pounds are in the ship's hold?"

Caroline carefully wrote *260, 95*, and *114* in a column on her slate. Since she dreamed of being captain of her own ship one day, she liked this type of problem. She began to add the numbers.

"Finished!" Rhonda declared.

Lydia put her slate pencil down. "Me too!"

"Let's give Caroline another moment," Mama said.

Caroline bent her head over her slate, trying to concentrate. Finally she wrote her answer. The little slate pencil made a scratchy sound.

"All right," Mama said. "What is the total?"

Lydia and Rhonda spoke at the same time. "Four hundred and sixty-nine."

Oh no, Caroline thought as she reluctantly displayed her slate. She'd written *369* at the bottom.

"You forgot to carry the one, Caroline," Mama said.

Lydia handed Caroline a rag. She rubbed the mistake from her slate. The warm feeling she'd had when the three girls had been planning Amelia's doll together was gone now. The error reminded Caroline that she was younger than Lydia and Rhonda. *It probably reminds them of that, too,* she thought.

"Very well, girls," Mama said. "That's all for today." She opened the stove door and added a log to the fire.

"I can tutor you in arithmetic, if you'd like," Rhonda told Caroline.

"It's kind of you to offer," Caroline said, trying to be polite without actually agreeing. She walked to the window and rubbed some frost from the glass so that she could peek outside. The fierce wind rattled the window and swirled snow in the air. She could barely make out the ships frozen into the harbor. As soon as the weather cleared, though, she knew that villagers would be outside with sleds, snowshoes, sleighs—

and best of all, Caroline thought, *ice skates!* Her spirits rose. She couldn't wait to be flying across the ice.

Behind her, Mama handed Lydia and Rhonda their cloaks. "Be sure to wrap up well," Mama said.

Rhonda shivered as she put on her bonnet. "Winter is harsh here by the lake."

"We've just had a run of bad weather," Caroline told her. "Winter can be great fun. You'll see!"

Lydia pulled on her thick woolen mittens. "Are you coming with us, Caroline?" she asked.

"I'll be along later," Caroline replied. "I'm going to help Mama for a while."

Standing at the window, Caroline watched Rhonda and Lydia head for home, leaning close and chattering together. Caroline sighed. "Rhonda and Lydia are better at sums than I am."

"They're also older than you are," Mama said gently. "You're doing well for someone who just turned ten."

"But I'm always the last to finish!" Caroline said.

Mama smoothed a strand of hair away from Caroline's forehead. "You're not used to having other students in class. I hope the fun of having two friends staying with us makes up for that."

"I do like having Rhonda and Lydia with us," Caroline said. "But sometimes . . . sometimes it feels as if Lydia and Rhonda are better friends with each other than they are with me."

"I'm sure that's not true," Mama said. She handed Caroline a small glass bottle of ink that had frozen overnight. "Now, please put this by the stove so that it can thaw while we eat."

Caroline and Mama shared a midday meal of baked beans and cornbread, brought from home in a tin bucket. When Mama went back to work, Caroline swept the office. Then she noticed that the woodbox was almost empty. She bundled up and went outside.

The shipyard was noisy and bustling as the men worked at top speed to build ships for the navy. Today two crews were sawing logs into planks with a *whizz-whizz* sound. Caroline smiled proudly. The workers had recently finished one gunboat, and they were already starting the next. Soon the new boat would take shape, right over there—

Caroline caught her breath. She could see clearly across the yard. The wind was no longer blowing snow about. Such fine, calm weather meant it was safe to go skating!

Caroline darted back into the office. "Mama, may I go skating?" She bounced on her toes. "Please? I'll ask Lydia and Rhonda to come along." Skating was surely something that all three of them could enjoy together!

"You may," Mama said. Then she gave Caroline a stern look. "As long as the other girls go with you, that is. Remember the rule."

"I won't forget," Caroline promised. She was not permitted to go out on the frozen lake by herself.

Caroline hurried home as fast as the drifted snow allowed. As she ran upstairs, she heard Lydia's and Rhonda's voices coming from her bedchamber. Caroline burst into the room. "The wind has died!" she announced.

"Thank goodness," Lydia said. She was holding Caroline's little mirror, watching as Rhonda arranged her hair.

"Mmm," Rhonda added. She had a hairpin pinched between her lips. She used it to pin a curl in place on top of Lydia's head.

Didn't the older girls understand? "That means we can go out on the lake," Caroline said.

"Why would we want to do that?" Rhonda asked.

"We can go skating!" Caroline explained happily.

"What do you think, Rhonda?" Lydia asked. "Shall we go skating?"

Caroline's smile slipped away. In the old days, the promise of sunshine and good ice would have made Lydia race Caroline out the front door.

"Not today, I don't think," Rhonda said. "I like fixing hair. I don't want to go outside in this cold anyway."

Lydia held out a picture of a woman wearing stylish clothes. "Your neighbor loaned us a copy of *The Lady's Magazine*," she told Caroline. "Rhonda is arranging my hair so that I look like the lady in this illustration. See?"

"And then Lydia's going to arrange *my* hair," Rhonda added. "We'll do yours too, if you want."

Caroline's shoulders slumped. How could Lydia and Rhonda think that arranging hair was more fun than skating? "No, thank you," she said. With a sigh, she left the older girls alone and headed back downstairs.

Caroline found Grandmother sitting by the kitchen fire with a pile of mending. Grandmother peered at her. "You look troubled, child."

Caroline dropped onto a bench. "I wanted to go skating this afternoon," she said.

"Why don't you, then?" Grandmother asked.

Caroline thumped her heel against the bench. "Because Rhonda and Lydia won't go with me."

"Ah." Grandmother nodded. "I wish I could take you, Caroline, but my skating days are long behind me." A faraway look came into her eyes. "I was a fine skater in my day, though. What fun it is to glide over the ice!"

"Oh, *yes*," Caroline said. She loved seeing sunlight glitter on ice. She loved breathing in the crisp, clean air. She loved flying over the frozen lake, free as a bird.

"Why don't you take Amelia sledding instead?" Grandmother asked. "I believe she's in the parlor with her mother."

Caroline sighed. "Amelia is too little to sled down a *real* hill," she told Grandmother. "I'd just have to pull her around. That wouldn't be any fun."

Grandmother looked down her nose at Caroline, then went back to her sewing.

That look made Caroline feel guilty. "I'll play with Amelia another time," she promised. "Today, I want to go skating with Lydia and Rhonda. But Rhonda doesn't want to." *And Rhonda's opinion seems to be more important to Lydia than my wishes,* Caroline couldn't help adding to herself.

Grandmother made a knot and snipped the thread. "Does Rhonda know how to skate?"

Caroline blinked. Didn't everyone know how to skate? "I . . . I didn't ask."

"Well, my girl," Grandmother said, "perhaps you should."

Caroline thought about that. Rhonda was new to Lake Ontario. Maybe she *didn't* know how to skate. *If that's true,* Caroline thought, *Lydia and I can teach her.* She grinned.

"Thank you, Grandmother," Caroline said. She already felt more cheerful. Soon she'd be out on the frozen lake with her friends—and for once, being the youngest wouldn't matter one bit.

Not Ladylike

C aroline ran out of the kitchen and back upstairs. In the bedroom, Rhonda was holding the mirror now. "Did you change your mind?" she asked. "Would you like us to fix your hair, too?"

"No, thank you," Caroline said. "Rhonda, do you know how to skate?"

Rhonda made a face. "I tried skating once. My ankles wobbled. I fell six times. I had bruises all over."

"Lydia and I can teach you!" Caroline offered.

Rhonda shook her head.

"Hold still!" Lydia cried. "Oh, I've made a snarl now. I need to comb it out and start over."

"Please, Rhonda?" Caroline asked. "Won't you try once more?"

"I don't have skates," Rhonda said.

Caroline had already thought of that. "You can borrow Mama's. They may be a little too big, but you can manage. It will be fun!"

"If the skates are too big, I'll be even more likely to fall." Rhonda sighed. "Besides, Caroline, we're already doing something fun."

Caroline's frustration popped out. "But it's silly to stay inside on such a sunny day!"

The room got quiet. Lydia and Rhonda exchanged a look in the mirror. Caroline waited, hoping one of them would say, *You're right, Caroline. It's a fine day for skating, and the three of us shouldn't waste it. Let's head out, all together.* But neither girl spoke. Finally Caroline turned around, left the room, and thumped down the stairs.

In the parlor, she went to the front window and looked out toward Lake Ontario. *Oh, Papa,* she thought, *where are you?* If Papa were here, *he* would understand how she felt.

The ache in Caroline's heart felt worse than ever. Papa loved to skate! He had taught Caroline when she was a little girl. On the first good day for skating the previous winter, Papa had been too busy to take

Caroline out on the ice. After supper, however, he'd told her to fetch her skates.

"But, Papa, the sun has gone down!" Caroline had protested.

"So it has," Papa had said, his eyes twinkling. "The moon is full, though." And off the two of them had gone. It had been magical to skate in the hush of night-time, with starlight glowing on the frozen lake and a bonfire blazing on shore to guide skaters home.

Caroline sighed, tucked that special memory away, and went back to the kitchen. "Rhonda doesn't know how to skate," she reported to Grandmother. "I said that Lydia and I could teach her, but she said no." Caroline dropped back on the bench. "That means I can't go."

Grandmother gave Caroline a look that seemed to say, *Come, Caroline, stop complaining. What are you going to do now?*

Caroline heard faint giggling from upstairs and glanced wistfully toward the sound. It would be so much fun to skate between Rhonda and Lydia! She imagined the three of them laughing and talking, maybe even racing each other back to the shore.

*I **know** the three of us can have fun together,* Caroline thought. Two days earlier the older girls had helped with Caroline's least favorite chore, baking bread. While scheming about Amelia's doll and giggling about flour on Lydia's nose, they'd made four tasty loaves. If they could enjoy a chore like baking, sharing winter games should be even better. Caroline stared at the fire. It shouldn't be so hard to convince the older girls to bundle up and head outdoors!

Well, I'm not giving up, she thought. They had a long winter ahead, and she wanted to enjoy it with Lydia and Rhonda.

"On days like this, I wish we could have lessons at home," Rhonda said the next morning as she bundled up to walk to the shipyard with Caroline and Lydia. "It's so cold!"

Caroline waved at a neighbor who was chopping firewood. "We just need to keep moving," she said. "At least it's sunny today." She liked the way sunshine flashed on the icicles hanging from every roof.

As the girls turned a corner, they heard shouts and

laughter coming from a group of boys who were sledding down a hill. "Caroline!" one of them called. "Want
to take a run?" He gestured to his sled.

"Yes!" Grinning, she turned to her companions.
"Let's all go!"

Rhonda shook her head. Lydia hesitated before saying, "We really don't have time."

Caroline frowned. Lydia had always loved to go
sledding! Caroline turned her back and hurried to the
top of the hill. When the other girls saw how fast she
went, perhaps they would change their minds.

"Watch me," Caroline called, settling on the sled.
She dug her heels into the snow and pushed off.
Whoosh! She laughed as the sled flew down the slope,
the wind stinging her cheeks.

She was almost to the bottom of the hill before she
saw that the boys had built up a wall of snow to keep
sledders from zooming into the road. She leaned back
and dug in her heels again, but she was going too fast
to stop.

The sled crashed into the snowbank. Caroline
flew from her sled. "Ooh!" she yelped as icy snow
slid under her collar. She didn't mind getting a little

snow down her neck, though. That ride was worth it.

"That was fun!" she called to the other girls. "Want to try?"

"It's time for lessons," Rhonda said.

Caroline gave the sled back to its owner and joined Rhonda and Lydia. "Mama won't mind if we're a few minutes late," she said. "Are you sure you don't want to take just one slide before we go to the shipyard?"

"Sledding isn't ladylike," Lydia said.

"You're covered with snow!" Rhonda added. "Gracious, Caroline."

Caroline brushed at her cloak with mittened hands. "It doesn't matter," she said. When had Lydia decided that she was too ladylike to go sledding? Why was Rhonda so worried about a tiny bit of snow?

"We really must go," Lydia said. "Come along, Caroline." She turned away, and Rhonda followed.

Caroline kicked some snow. *Lydia sounds as if she's my mother,* she thought, *instead of my cousin!*

After lessons Caroline told the older girls, "I'm going to stay here at the shipyard and help the men

unravel old rope to make caulk. Would you like
to help?"

Lydia and Rhonda exchanged a glance. "I don't
think so," Lydia said. "We'll see you at home later."
Rhonda nodded.

Well, fine, Caroline thought crossly. **I'm** *going to stay
and do something important.*

After sharing a noon meal with Mama, Caroline
left the office. In the carpentry shop, she found Hosea,
the sailmaker, sitting near a little stove. He was mending a torn piece of canvas. Jed, the youngest carpenter,
was carving wooden pegs that would help hold the
new gunboat together.

A third man, Richard, sat beside a mound of old
rope. "Come to help, Miss Caroline?" he asked.

"Yes," Caroline told him. She fetched an empty
workbasket, picked up one of the pieces of rope, and
settled on a little stool. Then she began picking the
rope apart.

Richard was a caulker. His job was to seal boats
so that not a drop of water could seep in. He made
something called oakum from the loose strands of old
rope. The oakum was mixed with sticky pitch from

pine trees. Richard hammered the mixture into the tiny cracks between wooden planks. Caroline loved knowing that *her* bits of rope would become part of a gunboat that would fight the British.

She worked steadily, listening as the men swapped stories. Her thoughts kept straying to Rhonda and Lydia, though. *Unraveling rope is important work—but I suppose it's not **ladylike** enough for them,* Caroline thought.

"Are you looking forward to Christmas, Miss Caroline?" Richard asked.

Caroline nodded, but her spirits drooped even lower. The holiday was only a few days away, and she still needed a gift for Rhonda. Teaching her to skate would make a good gift . . . but Rhonda had already said she didn't want to try again.

Suddenly Caroline sat up straight, her hands going still. What if she could give Rhonda a pair of new skates for Christmas? Beautiful skates, just her size. Rhonda liked pretty things, and having skates that fit her well might encourage her to try again.

As Caroline reached for a piece of rope, another idea flashed through her mind. *Rope—that's it!* she thought. *I could tie a rope around Rhonda's waist and tow her across the ice.* Rhonda didn't want to skate because she was afraid of falling. But with someone towing her—

The door opened, and Mr. Tate stepped in with a blast of cold air. "How is the work coming?" he asked.

"Just fine," Hosea said.

"Miss Caroline's been a big help today," Richard added.

Mr. Tate nodded with approval at the mound of rope fibers between Caroline and Richard.

Caroline jumped to her feet. "Pardon me," she said, "but I was wondering . . ." Her voice trailed away. Mr. Tate had a lot of responsibility at the shipyard. Perhaps she shouldn't ask for special favors.

"Yes, Miss Caroline?" He gave her an encouraging smile. Mr. Tate had worked for Caroline's parents for many years. He was more than a worker—he was a family friend.

"I'd like to give Rhonda a pair of skates for Christmas," Caroline explained. "I know all the men are very busy, but I was wondering if—"

"Of course!" Mr. Tate understood at once. "It

wouldn't take Joseph long to fashion the blades."
Joseph was the blacksmith.

"And I could make the leather straps," Hosea
offered. "I'll do it in the evening, sir," he added, looking
at Mr. Tate.

Caroline clapped her hands. "Oh, *thank* you!" She
beamed from one man to the other, bouncing on her
toes. With a towrope, she was certain she could help
Rhonda learn to glide over the ice. And she'd soon have
a beautiful new pair of skates to give her friend on
Christmas, too.

On the day before Christmas, someone knocked on
the front door just as Caroline finished paring potatoes
for Grandmother. Caroline opened the door. "Joseph,
come in from the cold!" she said. Despite his warm wool
coat and hat, the blacksmith's cheeks were bright red.

Joseph stamped snow from his shoes and stepped
inside. He held a bulky canvas bundle under one arm.
After greeting Grandmother, who was sitting by the
fire, he said in a hoarse whisper, "I've got the skates,
Miss Caroline."

"Ooh, let's see!" Caroline cried. "It's all right. Rhonda's off visiting her father today."

Joseph placed his bundle on the table and unwrapped a pair of skates.

Caroline's eyes widened. "Oh, *Joseph*!"

"I hope they suit," Joseph said. "Hosea and I worked from the tracing you made of Miss Rhonda's shoe, so the size should be just right."

Caroline examined the skates. The leather straps Hosea had made were soft and even. The blades Joseph had crafted were sharp and straight, and he'd added a fancy twist of iron on each toe. She looked from the delicate work to Joseph's huge hands and back again. "Those," she told him, "are surely the prettiest skates ever made."

"They are indeed," Grandmother agreed.

Joseph ducked his head, looking embarrassed. "I'm glad you think they'll do."

"Do?" Caroline grinned. "Rhonda is sure to love them!"

After bidding Joseph good-bye, Caroline picked up the skates. *At least . . . I hope Rhonda loves them*, she thought.

She took one last look at the skates before hiding them away in Grandmother's bedchamber. All Caroline could do now was wait to see if Rhonda was as delighted with the skates as *she* was.

Christmas

"C aroline?" Grandmother called. "Please carry this platter into the dining room." Christmas Day had come, and wonderful aromas had been drifting from the kitchen all day.

Caroline picked up the heavy platter and inhaled the rich scent of ham. For most of the year, only salted and smoked pork was available, but Grandmother had purchased a juicy fresh ham for Christmas dinner.

The dining room was crowded, but everyone managed to squeeze into place: Caroline, Mama, and Grandmother; Lydia, Aunt Martha, and Uncle Aaron; and Rhonda, Amelia, and their parents. All through the meal, the three older girls shared secret, excited looks. When Amelia saw the doll, would she be too surprised for words? Or would she chatter with excitement?

Caroline was confident that Amelia would like her gift. Would Rhonda be as happy with her beautiful new skates? Feeling hopeful, Caroline imagined Rhonda's face lighting with pleasure when she realized that Caroline had arranged to have them made just for *her*. Surely Rhonda wouldn't look down her nose and say "Gracious, Caroline!" then. Once Rhonda had her new skates and Lydia had the warm muff Caroline had made for her, there would be nothing to keep the three of them from having fun together on the ice.

Although Caroline had trouble sitting still, Christmas dinner was too wonderful to rush. Grandmother and Mrs. Hathaway served the ham with peas and potatoes. Aunt Martha had baked two apple pies and boiled cornmeal with sweet maple syrup to make hasty pudding.

After the feast, everyone moved into the parlor, and Uncle Aaron settled down with the Bible. This was the first time Papa hadn't been there to read the Christmas story, and Caroline felt a wave of longing as Uncle Aaron began. As she listened to the familiar words, she looked at the embroidered fire screen that she'd made for Papa. It sat by the hearth, waiting to welcome him home. *Merry Christmas, Papa,* she thought, *wherever you are. I miss you more than ever.*

When Uncle Aaron finished, he shut the Bible gently. For a moment everyone was quiet, as if tucking the comforting story into their hearts for another year. Then Caroline tiptoed to Mama. "May we give our gifts now?" she asked.

Mama smiled. "Of course, dear child."

Lydia and Rhonda jumped to their feet. The three girls had decided that Amelia's gift would be the first one given.

Rhonda's face glowed with anticipation. "Close your eyes, Amelia," she said, "and hold out your hands. No peeking!"

Amelia scrunched her eyes tightly shut and eagerly held out her hands. Lydia fetched the doll from its hiding place in a drawer. She, Rhonda, and Caroline crowded close to gently lay the doll in Amelia's hands.

Amelia's eyes flew open. *"Oh,"* she gasped. She stared at the doll as if she'd never seen one before.

"Happy Christmas," Caroline said.

Amelia didn't move, keeping the doll balanced on her palms. "She's for *me*?" she asked.

Lydia laughed, clearly delighted by Amelia's wonderment. "She is," she assured the little girl. "The three of us made her just for you."

Slowly, gently, Amelia cradled the doll close. "She's *beautiful*."

"You must be careful with her," Rhonda added.

"I will," Amelia promised. "Thank you!" She put the doll down long enough to give each of the older girls a hug. When Caroline felt Amelia's arms squeeze her around the waist, her heart almost overflowed. She'd never seen Amelia so happy. The glance she shared with Lydia and Rhonda was full of satisfaction. *We did that,* Caroline thought. *With a good idea and a few scraps of cloth and yarn, we made Amelia happy.*

Then Amelia ran around the room, showing her new doll to the adults. "You girls did a lovely job," Mama said.

Mrs. Hathaway nodded. "You did indeed," she agreed. "Even dyeing yarn that pretty shade of brown to make the hair."

Rhonda shared a secret smile with Caroline and Lydia. "Better brown than purple," she whispered.

Caroline tried not to giggle, but she couldn't help it.

Lydia elbowed her, which was her cousin's way of saying, *Stop it! Don't make me laugh too!*

"Be polite, girls," Grandmother said, but her eyes were twinkling.

Amelia cradled her doll while more gifts were presented. Lydia sighed with delight when she saw her new muff. "It's so soft and warm!" she told Caroline. "Thank you."

Caroline took a deep breath. *I hope Rhonda is as happy with her gift as Amelia and Lydia are with theirs,* she thought. She felt tingly inside, half nervous and half excited. "I have a gift for you as well," Caroline told Rhonda. "Close your eyes."

Caroline fetched the skates from their hiding place and set them in Rhonda's lap. Rhonda opened her eyes. She stared at the skates.

"Hosea and Joseph made them," Caroline told her. "They're just the right size for you. Aren't they beautiful?"

Rhonda nodded.

"I know you didn't enjoy skating when you tried it before," Caroline added quickly, "but I think I can help keep you from falling."

"Thank you," Rhonda said finally. And that was all. Caroline felt her heart slide toward her toes.

As the evening went by, Caroline received gifts of embroidery silk, a new needle case, and warm woolen stockings. When she passed out the handkerchiefs she'd made, the adults all praised her handiwork. "I was in sore need of a new handkerchief," Uncle Aaron declared.

Rhonda, however, wouldn't meet her gaze at all. And when Caroline looked at Lydia, her cousin quickly glanced away, as if embarrassed for her.

Caroline blinked, trying not to cry. Christmas was ruined.

That night Caroline lay in bed, listening to the two older girls whisper from their cornhusk mattresses on the floor nearby. *Perhaps I should forget about having fun with them,* Caroline thought miserably.

She wished she'd explained her towrope plan when she presented the skates. Surely that would have put Rhonda's fears to rest! Maybe Rhonda loved the new skates but didn't show it because she was still afraid of falling. As Caroline finally drifted off to sleep, she knew what she needed to do.

The morning after Christmas dawned clear and cold. After breakfast, Caroline found Lydia and Rhonda in the parlor. "Mama has excused us from lessons today," Caroline began. "And it's a perfect morning for skating." She quickly explained her plan.

"You want to tow me over the ice?" Rhonda asked. "I don't think that will keep me from falling."

"No, wait," Lydia said thoughtfully. "It might work."

Caroline gave her cousin a grateful smile before turning back to Rhonda. "Getting started is the hardest part of learning to skate," she told her. "Getting a tow will help you build up speed."

Rhonda twisted her fingers together. "I don't know," she said.

"Skating really is great fun," Lydia told Rhonda. "With a little practice, you'll glide all over the ice."

"Please, Rhonda?" Caroline said. "Will you give skating one more try?"

"Oh, very well," Rhonda said reluctantly. "I'll try."

The girls dressed in their warmest clothes, gathered up their skates, and walked to the harbor. Lots of other people were already skating on the frozen lake—some hesitant, others with great speed and grace. A few skated near the navy ships, but Caroline didn't want to go there. Sailors had chopped trenches in the ice around their ships so that spies or enemy soldiers couldn't walk across the frozen lake and sneak aboard. *We mustn't take Rhonda anywhere near open water,* she thought.

"Let's go over there," she said, pointing to an area that was well away from the ships and most of the other skaters.

"Are you sure the ice is safe?" Rhonda asked.

"Yes," Caroline said firmly. "Bad ice looks dark. Thick ice has a nice white color, like this. See?"

Then she pointed toward a man and woman using a chair sled nearby. The man was skating and pushing his sweetheart along while she sat on the sled's cushioned seat. "That chair sled is a lot heavier than we are, and the ice is holding them up," she added.

"I've even seen horse-drawn sleighs pass through here." Lydia smiled reassuringly.

Rhonda squared her shoulders. "All right, then. I'm ready."

Caroline and Lydia strapped on their own skates and helped Rhonda put on hers. "Before you start, watch how I do it," Caroline told her friend. She pushed off on the ice. With just a few strokes, she felt as if she were flying!

Before going too far, though, she slowed reluctantly and returned to shore. "See?" she said to Rhonda. "You'll soon be skating like that too."

Caroline had borrowed a rope from the shipyard. While Lydia tied one end around Rhonda's waist, Caroline knotted the other end around her own. Lydia and Caroline helped Rhonda to her feet. Then they slowly moved onto the ice.

"My ankles are shaking already," Rhonda said.

"Hold on to my arm," Lydia offered. "Caroline, start pulling!"

Caroline pushed off on one foot. *"Oof,"* she gasped as the towrope tightened around her waist. Towing Rhonda was harder than she'd expected.

She wasn't about to give up, though. She dug the blade of one skate into the ice and shoved off harder. That sent her forward a few inches. She pushed off again with her other foot.

"Faster!" Lydia called.

I'm trying, Caroline thought. Summoning every bit of her strength, she kept skating forward. They all began to move a little more quickly.

Lydia tried to encourage Caroline and Rhonda. "That's the way!"

Caroline clenched her teeth and chanted silently, *Push off with the left foot, push off with the right.* The ice had some bumps, but she tried to avoid them. Gradually, as she picked up speed, it grew a little easier to keep skating.

"I'm doing it!" Rhonda exclaimed. "I'm really skating!"

Rhonda sounded so happy that Caroline dared a look over her shoulder. Rhonda was taking little strokes herself. "Isn't this fun?" Caroline called. Rhonda nodded.

Caroline looked ahead again—and saw a ridge in the ice, right in front of her. She gave a little hop, easily clearing the rough spot, but she knew that Rhonda wasn't ready to make such a move. "Watch out!" Caroline yelled.

Too late! Rhonda tripped and fell, pulling Lydia

down with her. Caroline felt a hard jerk on the rope. She banged down on the ice and slid backward into the other girls.

"Ow," Rhonda whimpered. She sat up slowly, rubbing her left elbow. Caroline was horrified to see tears in Rhonda's eyes.

"I'm sorry!" Caroline cried. "There was a bump in the ice, and I didn't see it in time. Next time I will—"

"No," Rhonda said. She pulled off her gloves and began fumbling with her skates. "I tried, Caroline. Just as I promised. But I *told* you I didn't think this would work. I don't want to fall down anymore. I shall walk back to shore."

Caroline looked at Lydia, hoping her cousin would say something to change Rhonda's mind. But Lydia didn't speak. Caroline silently untied the towrope. All three girls got to their feet.

Caroline struggled to hold frustration and disappointment inside. If only she'd spotted the ridge in time! Perhaps if she had, Rhonda wouldn't have fallen. *And if Rhonda hadn't fallen*, Caroline thought, *we all could have had fun on the lake.*

Caroline felt a heaviness settle in her heart as she

took one last, longing look toward the other skaters skimming over the ice. She'd hardly gotten to skate at all!

Even worse, Rhonda was clearly more unhappy with Caroline than ever.

When Caroline entered her bedchamber that evening, she found Rhonda and Lydia in their nightgowns, brushing their hair. Caroline tried not to look at the beautiful skates she'd given Rhonda, which had been dropped in a corner.

A fierce wind seemed determined to sneak in around the windowpanes. "*Brrr!* I'm going to sleep in my shawl tonight," Lydia said. She wrapped her woolen shawl around her shoulders and quickly slid beneath her blankets.

Rhonda did the same thing, and once she was settled, she pulled her blanket up to her chin. "I wish it were spring," she said.

Caroline, busy undressing, didn't answer. If Rhonda was going to be unhappy until spring came, she'd be unhappy for a long time.

"It's so nice to be outside in warm weather," Rhonda continued. Her voice sounded dreamy and she closed her eyes, as if imagining herself into a fine spring day. "Back in Albany, my friends and I had tea parties outside, or we went to the green for hoop races."

"That sounds lovely," Lydia said wistfully.

"I like racing hoops too," Caroline said. She blew out the lamp and slid into bed. "Last year we had hoop races in the village on Independence Day." It had been great fun to roll big wooden hoops over the grass, while little children practiced nearby.

Suddenly, Caroline sat up as a new idea popped into her head. "We don't have to wait until spring to race hoops. We could race hoops on the snow!"

"Oh, Caroline," Lydia said in that I'm-older-and-smarter-than-you tone that Caroline particularly disliked. "Hoops would just sink in the snow!"

"Today's sunshine made the snow melt a little," Caroline pointed out, "so there will likely be a glaze of ice over everything tomorrow. I know a hill just outside of town that would be perfect for hoop races!"

"But we don't have hoops," Rhonda said.

"We can borrow some from the shipyard," Caroline

promised. "I've seen spare wheel rims in the blacksmith shop. So, what do you think?" She held her breath, hoping that Rhonda and Lydia wouldn't dismiss this idea too.

"I think we should try it!" Lydia agreed. Her voice had lost its bossy tone. She sounded excited.

Caroline waited for Rhonda to respond.

"Yes, that does sound like fun," Rhonda said finally. "And I won't have to worry about falling down."

Caroline snuggled back under the covers. She could hardly wait for morning.

Danger on the Ice

T he next day, after lessons with Mama, Caroline told Lydia and Rhonda to head home without her. "I'll be along shortly," she promised. "I need to see the blacksmith."

She found Joseph working at his forge, shaping hot iron into a tool. "Excuse me," Caroline said, staying a safe distance from the forge as Papa had taught her. "Might I borrow some cartwheel rims?" She pointed toward one of the shop's dim corners, which was cluttered with all sorts of stray metal pieces and tools.

Joseph lay down his hammer. "Whatever for?"

"Lydia and Rhonda and I want to have hoop races," Caroline explained.

"I've got two small ones," Joseph said. "You're welcome to borrow them."

Caroline collected the two narrow iron rims, each about waist-high, and headed for home. *We need three hoops,* she thought, *or it won't be any fun.* She tried to think. Suddenly she smiled. She knew where there was another hoop.

When she got home, Caroline headed for the family's storeroom, where Grandmother's spinning wheel sat among traveling trunks and old pieces of furniture. Grandmother hadn't had any wool to work with in months, so the spinning wheel was dusty. It was made almost entirely from wood, but it had a narrow iron rim to hold the wheel together. The unheated storeroom was so cold and dry that the wooden wheel had shrunk a little. When Caroline pulled on the iron rim, it easily slid from the wheel. She grinned. Perfect!

With the hoop in hand, Caroline hurried downstairs and joined the other girls. "I've got three hoops," she said triumphantly. "We're all set."

Once they left home, Caroline led the way down the lane, away from the busiest streets. With so many new ships and forts and storehouses being built, men had cut trees all around the village. Logs, planks, and bricks were piled here and there, ready for work crews.

The girls took a footpath out of the village and soon arrived at a quiet, sloping meadow. "See?" Caroline said, her breath puffing white in the cold air. "There's a nice crust on the snow."

Lydia considered the slope. "We won't be able to run alongside our hoops in this snow," she said.

"I thought we could launch the hoops from the top of the hill," Caroline said. "We can all send our hoops down at the same time. The first hoop to reach the bottom is the winner." She pointed. The gentle slope stretched down to the lakeshore, but a fallen tree at the bottom—now covered with snow—would keep the hoops from rolling onto the ice.

"That's a good idea," Rhonda agreed. She pulled her scarf more snugly around her neck. "Ooh, that wind is chilly. I wish the sun were out today."

"We'll stay warm as long as we keep moving," Lydia promised. "Let's line up here, on the hilltop."

The three girls positioned their hoops. "Ready?" Rhonda called. "Go!"

Caroline sent her hoop sailing, but it quickly fell over. Keeping a hoop going on the slick slope was tricky!

"This is harder than racing hoops on grass," Lydia

gasped as the girls trudged back up the hill after their third try.

"I almost had it," Caroline said. "Next time my hoop will surely reach the bottom."

"Perhaps," Rhonda said with a teasing smile, "but *my* hoop is going to beat yours!"

As Caroline positioned her hoop for the next launch, she paused to enjoy the cold air against her face and the sound of footsteps crunching on snow. Rhonda's cheeks were flushed pink, and her eyes sparkled. Lydia laughed as she struggled the last few steps to the starting line. *Finally!* Caroline thought. She wanted to cheer.

This time, Lydia's hoop rolled all the way to the bottom of the hill. It hit the fallen log and fell over. "I win!" she crowed.

"This time you do," Rhonda informed her, "but Caroline and I will catch up to you!"

Soon all three girls were able to keep their hoops rolling. "Let's start keeping count," Lydia suggested. "If your hoop hits that little rise first, you win a point."

For some time the count stayed close. Each girl had a chance to cheer as her hoop reached the target first. Slowly, though, Caroline fell behind.

It doesn't matter, she tried telling herself, but she couldn't help wanting to win—or at least catch up! After coming in last three times in a row, she paused at the top of the slope, thinking. She was using the hoop from the spinning wheel, which was not as heavy as the others. Perhaps she just needed to push her hoop harder.

"Ready?" Rhonda called again. "*Go!*"

Caroline launched her hoop with all her strength. The three hoops rolled down the slope, faster and faster. Caroline's hoop stayed out in front. "I'm going to win this time!" she cried. She clapped as her hoop sailed to the bottom.

Instead of falling over, though, the hoop kept spinning. It rolled right up the snow mound that covered the log. Then a gust of wind grabbed the hoop, carrying it over the rise and out of sight. Caroline's excitement turned to dismay as her hoop disappeared.

The three girls stared, open-mouthed. "My goodness!" Rhonda said.

They scrambled down the slope and over the log. Caroline stared at the frozen lake. "Where's the hoop?" she asked. "Do you see it?"

"No," Lydia said. Rhonda shook her head.

Caroline scanned the ice, looking this way and that. She couldn't see the iron hoop anywhere.

"The wind must have taken it a long way," Rhonda said at last.

Caroline lifted her chin. "Well then," she said, "we need to go out on the lake and look for it."

Lydia frowned. "Caroline, no! We don't know if the ice is safe here."

"I can tell if ice is safe," Caroline protested.

"*No*," Lydia said. "We're out of sight from the village. We mustn't go out there."

Caroline rubbed her mittened hands together anxiously. "I can't leave the hoop behind," she told the other girls. "It's the rim to Grandmother's spinning wheel."

Lydia's eyes went wide. "Did you ask permission before taking it?"

"No," Caroline admitted. "Do you think Grandmother will be angry with us?"

"Perhaps you should have thought about that before taking her hoop," Lydia said. "Honestly, Caroline!"

"Stop scolding me!" Caroline burst out. "I wouldn't

have taken the hoop if you two had been more friendly lately."

Lydia planted her hands on her hips. "This has nothing to do with Rhonda and me. You're the one who took the hoop."

"Stop it!" Rhonda cried. "Arguing won't help anything." She looked at Caroline. "You'll have to tell your grandmother what you did."

The other girls' scolding just made Caroline feel stubborn. "What I *have* to do," she retorted, "is find the hoop. It couldn't have gone too far."

"We're *not* going out on that ice," Rhonda insisted.

"I agree," Lydia added. "Listen, Caroline, we're older than you, and—"

"I don't care if you're older than me!" Caroline yelled. "I know how to read ice. I'm going to look for that hoop whether you like it or not."

Lydia and Rhonda exchanged a troubled glance.

"Are you coming with me?" Caroline demanded. She stared at the other girls, daring them to say no.

No one spoke.

"Fine," Caroline said. "I'll go by myself." She turned away. Her hands were shaking, and her stomach felt upset. *But I can't change my mind now*, she thought. She turned her back, straightened her shoulders, and walked onto the ice.

Caroline hadn't taken more than three steps before Lydia said, "Caroline, wait. I'll come with you."

"Me too," Rhonda said with a heavy sigh.

Caroline blew out a long, relieved breath. "Thank you," she said with frosty politeness.

Looking over the lake, Caroline felt a whisper of unease. Was she doing the right thing? What would Papa think if he could see her now? She'd *thought* she was becoming the steady person Papa wanted her to be. She didn't feel that way now.

I made a mistake by taking the hoop without permission, Caroline thought, *but I'm trying to be responsible and bring it back. That **is** the right thing to do . . . isn't it?* One thing was certain—she needed to remember everything Papa had taught her about safety on the frozen lake.

She turned and stepped back on the shore. Then she poked among the trees until she found three long, stout sticks. She handed one to Rhonda. "Carry this so that it's even with the ice," she told Rhonda.

Rhonda looked confused. "Why?"

"Wind can shift the ice and cause cracks," Caroline explained. Seeing the look of alarm on Rhonda's face, she continued quickly, "But you usually have warning. When the ice cracks, it sounds like a pistol shot. If a crack *did* open in the ice and you fell through, the stick would catch on the ice and keep you from drowning."

"People hardly ever fall in," Lydia added, but she looked nervous. She took her stick. "Let's get started."

The girls stepped onto the ice. Caroline peered into the distance until her eyes ached. She could hardly tell where the ice ended and the sky began. Everything looked gray. *That hoop has to be out here somewhere,* she told herself. At least the ice was good—thick and white. The day was growing colder, though. Wind raced across the frozen lake. Caroline's fingers and toes were soon numb despite her thick woolen mittens and socks.

"We're getting awfully far from shore," Lydia said finally. "We should turn back—"

"I *see* it!" Caroline cried. "It's just ahead." She began to hurry.

Suddenly Lydia yelled, "*Stop!* The ice is broken up there!"

Looking up, Caroline saw that they were reaching the end of a solid ice shelf that stretched from shore. The hoop lay near the shelf's edge. Just beyond, big pieces of ice bobbed lightly. Jagged ribbons of open water appeared and disappeared between the cakes of ice as they jostled together.

Caroline swallowed hard, trying to read the ice as Papa had taught her. "I can still get the hoop."

"Caroline, do not go any farther," Lydia ordered. "I *forbid* you to take one more step."

"I'll be careful," Caroline protested.

Rhonda grabbed Caroline's arm. "Don't you dare," she said. "Lydia's right."

Caroline clenched her teeth. She was not going to permit Lydia and Rhonda to order her around—not when she was so close to the hoop! "I know what I'm doing," she insisted. "You two stay here. I'm the lightest."

Ignoring the other girls' warnings, Caroline began walking forward, step by careful step. She tapped the ice ahead of her with the stick, checking for any sign of weakness. She pushed her hat back, uncovering her ears even though they prickled with cold. If the ice cracked, she wanted to hear it.

One step. Another. One more. Caroline concentrated on her goal. Three more steps. She was there! Caroline stooped and grabbed the iron hoop. *I have it!* she thought triumphantly.

As she rose to her feet, an extra-sharp blast of wind almost knocked her back down. Then came a deafening *cra-a-acking* sound, loud as a gunshot. The ice lurched beneath Caroline's feet. She struggled to keep her balance.

"*Caroline!*" Lydia shrieked.

Caroline looked back toward shore and was horrified to see a narrow channel of water, black and threatening, open between her and the main ice shelf. She stood now on a loose piece of ice about the size of her bedroom floor.

"Can you jump over the water?" Rhonda cried.

"No," Caroline called fearfully. "This piece of ice is staying balanced because I'm right in the middle of it." If she moved toward the edge, her weight might tip the ice over—and she'd plunge into the freezing water.

Lydia and Rhonda began a conversation that Caroline couldn't hear, with lots of pointing and gesturing. Caroline knew that Lydia would keep Rhonda safe. Lydia knew as much about ice as Caroline did. *No, Lydia knows **more** than I do,* Caroline admitted miserably. She'd made a terrible decision. Now she was in terrible trouble.

She tried to think, but her brain felt like slush. Fear made it hard to breathe. What if the wind pushed all these loose pieces farther away from land? "Help me!" she pleaded, blinking back tears. "I don't know what to do!"

"Caroline!" Lydia called. "Crouch down."

For once, Caroline was very glad to get an order from her cousin. She obeyed.

Lydia continued, "Now, stretch out on your stomach."

Caroline slowly stretched out on the ice, gasping each time it wobbled beneath her. Despite her thick coat, lying on the ice sent a deeper chill into her bones.

On the main ice shelf, Lydia lay down in the same manner. Then she inched her way over the ice toward the crack. Rhonda held on to Lydia's ankles, ready to yank her back if the ice gave way.

Lydia stopped when she was near the edge of the ice shelf. Then she extended her stick slowly across the water and over the ice cake toward Caroline. "Grab the end!"

Caroline snaked her hand forward and grasped the end of Lydia's stick. "Don't try to pull me over," Caroline begged. "I'll fall into the water!"

"I'm just going to hang on," Lydia promised, "while Rhonda goes for help."

Knowing that Lydia was at the other end of the stick made Caroline feel a little better. At least she wasn't going to drift away.

As she watched Rhonda hurry off, Caroline tried to slow her racing heart. Lydia was in a bad spot too. What if the ice Lydia was lying on broke away as well? *Lydia is risking her own safety to help me,* Caroline thought with a new stab of fear. In fact, both Rhonda and Lydia had taken a great risk when they followed her onto the ice. Caroline felt tears brim over and freeze on her cheeks. She'd made many mistakes that day. No wonder the older girls didn't always listen to her ideas!

Caroline didn't know how long she lay shivering on the ice, clutching Lydia's stick, before she heard a distant shout. Rhonda appeared on the shore. But . . .

she was alone! Caroline's hopes sank. Why hadn't Rhonda brought help?

Then she saw that Rhonda was dragging a long plank of wood. "I found a board," Caroline heard Rhonda say.

"Good," Lydia replied. "Lay it on the ice, and then slide it over the water to Caroline's piece of ice. Carefully!"

Rhonda placed the board on the ice shelf and gently pushed it forward. One end came to rest right beside Caroline.

"Caroline," Lydia called, "we'll hold down this end of the plank so you can walk across."

Moving as slowly and steadily as possible, Caroline began to rise to her feet. She had to let go of Lydia's stick so that she could use both arms to help keep her balance. Each time the ice bobbed beneath her, she caught her breath. Finally she was standing upright, but although the plank rested right beside her boots, she couldn't seem to take a step.

Caroline looked at her cousin. "What if the plank pushes my cake of ice underwater?"

"It won't," Lydia promised.

With a deep breath, Caroline stepped onto the board. It was very narrow. She took one last glance at the hoop. She wanted to grab it, but she was afraid that carrying it might throw her off balance.

Caroline began to walk along the plank, placing each foot carefully. Her legs trembled with cold and fright. She waved her arms wildly to keep from falling off the board.

When she reached the channel that had opened in the ice and saw the dark water moving restlessly below her, she froze with terror. If she lost her balance, she'd fall into Lake Ontario. The icy water would soak her heavy clothing, making it impossible for her to swim. Her hands would be too numb to grab Lydia's stick. The older girls wouldn't be able to save her.

"Almost there!" Lydia called.

Rhonda added, "You can do it, Caroline!"

Their encouragement gave Caroline the strength she needed to take another step. *Keep going*, she told herself. *Don't stop moving. Don't look down. Just keep going.*

It seemed to take forever to inch over the open water. Finally Caroline moved past the channel. She'd reached the ice shelf. She was safe.

Fast Friends

Lydia burst into tears, threw her arms around Caroline, and pulled her away from the edge. Caroline clung to her cousin as they walked toward the shore. Now that she was safe, she couldn't stop shaking.

"I was so frightened!" Lydia cried.

"I thought we'd lost you," Rhonda added, her voice cracking.

Caroline stepped back and looked from one girl to the other. "Th-thank you," she said through chattering teeth. "And—I'm s-sorry. I know I put us all in danger. I should never have gone out on the ice."

"We tried to say so," Lydia reminded her. "Why didn't you listen?"

It was hard to tell the truth, but Caroline knew she had to try. "Sometimes you two treat me like a little child," she said. "You never think about what *I* want to do. It makes me feel left out."

"*We* don't leave you out," Rhonda protested. "When we invite you to do things with us, you act as if you think we're silly."

I do? Caroline wondered. A flush warmed her cheeks. Was it possible that she might have hurt the other girls' feelings in much the same way that they'd hurt hers? "I don't think you're silly," Caroline said. "I just wanted us to have some fun together outdoors."

She looked at Rhonda. "I gave you those beautiful skates for Christmas, and you didn't even want to try them."

"I'd already told you that I didn't *like* skating," Rhonda said quietly. "Those skates weren't a gift to me, Caroline. They were a gift you gave yourself."

Caroline stared at her friend. What an awful thing to say! *But . . . it's true,* she realized. She blew out a long breath before admitting, "You're right."

Rhonda squeezed Caroline's hand. "I'm sorry that I hurt your feelings. I never meant to."

"I'm sorry, too," Lydia said quickly.

Caroline felt as if a heavy block of ice had just

slipped from her shoulders. "And I am as well," she said. "Now, let's go home."

When the girls got home, Caroline said, "You two go change into dry clothes. I'll be along."

"What are you going to do?" Lydia asked.

"I need to find Grandmother," Caroline told them. "I have some explaining to do."

It was hard to confess to Grandmother. Caroline ended the tale by saying, "I'm sorry, Grandmother. *Very* sorry." She stood with her back to the hearth. The fire's warmth was lovely. The hard look in Grandmother's eyes was terrible.

"What are you sorry about?" Grandmother asked.

Everything! Caroline started to say, but she realized that Grandmother expected something more. "I'm sorry I took the rim from your spinning wheel without asking your permission," Caroline began. "And for going out on the ice. And for talking Lydia and Rhonda into going with me."

Grandmother's face did not soften. "You've made a lot of poor decisions, Caroline."

"Yes, ma'am." Caroline stared at the floor. "I didn't even bring back the rim for your spinning wheel," she added miserably.

"Hmm," Grandmother said. "At least you made one good choice. I'd much rather lose the hoop than lose *you*."

Those words made Caroline feel a tiny bit better.

"And we can easily get a new hoop made," Grandmother added. "But, Caroline, you must *never* again let hurt feelings lead you to make foolish—even dangerous—decisions."

"I won't," Caroline promised. She added silently, *And I'll try not to let my feelings get hurt so easily.* What was done couldn't be undone, but from now on she'd try to consider *other* people's feelings, too.

Thinking about that, Caroline looked away and noticed Amelia standing by the window, watching some boys passing by with their sleds. She had a look of longing on her face.

"Amelia," Caroline said, "would you like me to take you outside? I could pull you around on my sled."

Amelia stared at her with surprise. "Oh, yes!"

Grandmother gave Caroline a tiny nod of approval.

Five minutes later, Caroline began towing Amelia across the garden on her sled. The little girl clapped her hands and giggled with delight. "This is fun!"

Caroline thought, *I get frustrated because I'm younger than Lydia and Rhonda, but Amelia's the youngest of all and doesn't have anyone to play with.* Caroline wished she'd offered to take Amelia sledding long ago.

"There's a little hill behind the neighbors' house," Caroline called over her shoulder. "They won't mind if we sled there. Would you like to try that?"

"Let's *go!*" Amelia shouted.

Caroline smiled. Perhaps she'd found a friend for outdoor adventures—at least small ones—after all.

New Year's Day—January 1, 1813—dawned clear and cold. After breakfast Caroline went into the parlor and sat by the map she'd stitched for Papa. Where was he, right this minute? Was he somewhere represented on her map, or had the British taken him far, far away? *It's a brand-new year, Papa,* Caroline thought. Surely he would come home in 1813. He simply *had* to.

Lydia poked her head through the door. "I've been

looking for you, Caroline," she said. "Would you like to go skating? Just you and me."

Caroline stared at her cousin. "But . . . won't Rhonda feel left out?" she asked.

"We three don't have to do everything together," Lydia said. Her eyes twinkled. "Rhonda won't mind, I promise."

"Then yes!" Caroline agreed. She raced for the door but then skidded to a halt. "Would you mind if we invite Amelia? She can wear the skates I used when I was little."

Lydia nodded. "That's a fine idea."

Amelia thought that was a fine idea, too. "You'll take *me*?" she squealed. "Thank you!"

Soon Caroline, Lydia, and Amelia had bundled into their warmest clothes and set off for the lake. When Amelia saw other skaters gliding this way and that, she jumped up and down with excitement.

Caroline laughed. "You'll have to stand still long enough for us to put on your skates, Amelia."

The two older girls put on their own skates before strapping the smallest pair onto Amelia's boots. "Caroline and I will hold you up," Lydia promised.

"Let us pull you along at first, so you get the feel of the ice."

"We'll stay off to one side, where there are fewer people," Caroline added.

Amelia held herself stiffly at first, but she relaxed as the older girls pulled her along. Soon Lydia said, "Try taking some little strokes. Watch my feet. See how I push off against the ice?"

Caroline felt Amelia's hand squeezing hers even tighter as the little girl tried to copy Lydia's movements. "That's it!" Caroline cried. "You're skating!" Amelia nodded proudly.

Then Caroline heard a familiar voice. "My goodness!" Rhonda called. "I didn't expect to see my little sister learning to skate today too!"

Caroline whipped her head around. What she saw made her dig one skate blade into the ice and come to a quick halt. She stared, open-mouthed with surprise. Lydia laughed with delight.

Rhonda, wearing her new skates, wobbled to a stop nearby. She was pushing a small chair sled. Grandmother sat in the chair, wrapped in blankets. Her face was glowing.

"I got the idea that day I came out on the ice with you," Rhonda told Caroline. "With your mother's permission, Lydia and I asked Mr. Tate if he'd allow a couple of the shipyard workers to make this chair sled. The handles are nice and strong. As long as I hold on to them, I won't fall down."

"And I," Grandmother added, "am out on the ice for the first time in years!"

"It's a *wonderful* idea," Caroline said.

Amelia tugged Caroline's hand. "I want to ride in the sled."

"Come sit on my lap, child," Grandmother offered. Lydia and Caroline helped Amelia get settled. Grandmother arranged the blankets so that they covered them both.

With a look of determination, Rhonda began skating again, pushing the sled in front of her. "Have fun," she called to Lydia and Caroline. "Soon I'll be able to keep up with you!"

Caroline waved them away with a smile. Somehow, despite the terrible mistakes she'd made recently, everything had turned out well. *Maybe staying steady doesn't mean never making mistakes*, she thought. Maybe the most important thing was to try to learn from mistakes, and do better next time.

"Come on, Caroline," Lydia called. "I'll race you!"

Caroline grinned. "Let's *go!*" she shouted, and pushed off as hard as she could. She marveled at the beauty of sunlight glittering on the snowy shore. She breathed in the crisp, clean air. And soon she was flying over the frozen lake, free as a bird.

Oh, Papa, how you would love this! Caroline thought. For a moment, tears blurred the shore, and longing squeezed her heart until she could hardly breathe with wishing he were home.

Then Caroline blinked away her tears and looked out across the great lake. She filled her lungs with fresh, cold air. *I'll stay steady, just as I promised you,* she told Papa. The blade of her skate made a sharp, clear sound against the ice as she pushed off again. *I'll stay steady for as long as it takes. Until you're home again and we're flying over the lake together.*

INSIDE Caroline's World

Caroline Abbott lives in Sackets Harbor, New York, at the edge of Lake Ontario, a lake so big that it looks like an ocean. In the early 1800s, the land around the Great Lakes was covered in forests. Villages like Sackets Harbor were remote and isolated, far from cities like New York.

Shipbuilders like Caroline's father had good reason to be proud of the ships they built. The tall ships that sailed the Great Lakes were an impressive sight, with white sails billowing in the breeze. Most roads were barely better than muddy paths, so it was difficult, slow, and expensive to carry goods by wagon. Boats moved more quickly and could carry much more cargo. For this reason, most early towns were built near water. Ships delivered useful items such as dishes and fabric, as well as luxuries like mirrors, fancy dolls, and even pianos.

When Caroline was a girl, America was young, too. It had just eighteen states. But the country was growing fast. Its population had almost doubled since the end of the Revolutionary War, thirty years before. Its land now swept from the Atlantic Ocean to the Rocky Mountains.

Many Americans were pleased with their country's rapid growth, but Britain was not. The two countries were on bad terms. The British knew that some Americans wanted to take control of British colonies in Canada. And many Americans believed that Britain was encouraging Indians to fight American settlers.

Even worse, ever since the Revolutionary War, the British had captured American sailors at sea and forced them to serve in the British navy. Over the years, more than 10,000 men had been kidnapped. More recently, the British had begun to block American ships from landing in other countries to trade, making it much harder for American farmers and businessmen to earn a living.

Finally, on June 18, 1812, the United States declared war. The news traveled slowly, however, and many sailors were caught off guard, just like Caroline's father.

The United States was not prepared to fight Britain, which had the world's most powerful navy. Only one U.S. warship patrolled the vast waters of Lake Ontario. But the Americans knew that the British had to cross Lake Ontario to get supplies to their forts on the Great Lakes. Whoever controlled Lake Ontario would control a key supply route—and could win the war. America needed more ships, and fast.

More than a thousand shipbuilders, sailmakers, carpenters, and sailors hurried to Sackets Harbor to help build and sail a fleet. A small shipyard like Abbott's would suddenly have become extremely busy!

The war changed life in Sackets Harbor. The streets were filled with strangers. The air was filled with the sounds of sawing and hammering. A girl gazing out over the lake would no longer see only peaceful ships bringing goods from far away. Now she would see fierce warships fitted with rows of cannons ready to do battle.

Read more of CAROLINE'S stories,
available from booksellers and at *americangirl.com*

≥ *Classics* ≤
Caroline's classic series, now in two volumes:

Volume 1:
Captain of the Ship
When war breaks out and
Papa is captured, Caroline
must learn to steer a steady
course without him.

Volume 2:
Facing the Enemy
The war comes closer and
closer to Sackets Harbor. Can
Caroline make the right decision
when the enemy attacks?

≥ *Journey in Time* ≤
Travel back in time—and spend a day with Caroline.

Catch the Wind
Go sailing with Caroline, help raiders capture an enemy fort,
or ride an American warship to a hidden bay! Choose your
own path through this multiple-ending story.

≥ *Mysteries* ≤
More thrilling adventures with Caroline!

Traitor in the Shipyard
Caroline suspects one of Papa's trusted workers is an enemy spy.

The Traveler's Tricks
Caroline and Rhonda ride a stagecoach—right into trouble!

≥ A Sneak Peek at ≤

Facing the Enemy

A Caroline Classic
Volume 2

Caroline's adventures continue in the
second volume of her classic stories.

aroline and Mama made their way back to the harbor. Suddenly Caroline heard a faint rattle of musket fire in the distance.

"I don't like the sound of that," Mama said grimly.

"How could there be fighting already?" Caroline burst out. "I thought the British were stuck offshore!" Were British soldiers already marching toward Sackets Harbor? Caroline shivered. They had no way of knowing what was happening even a few miles away.

"Perhaps the British got tired of waiting and rowed some men ashore," Mama said. "If so, they can't have landed many soldiers. Still, we must hurry." She grabbed Caroline's arm as they elbowed their way toward the yard. Caroline was glad to feel Mama's firm grasp.

When they reached Abbott's again, Caroline expected to see the workers still standing guard. Instead, the men had gathered in a clump near the entrance. Mr. Tate seemed to be arguing with a man in an American military uniform. *Oh no,* Caroline thought. *What now?*

Mama hurried to join the conversation. Caroline wanted to hear, too, and followed on Mama's heels.

Caroline could tell by the fancy braid on the soldier's coat that he was an officer. He had gray hair, and there were dark circles beneath his eyes.

"Gentlemen!" Mama said in a tone that stopped the discussion. She introduced herself to the officer. "I'm in charge of the shipyard when my husband is away," she told him. "What's happening?" She gestured toward the far-off sound of muskets.

"A few dozen British men and some of their Indian allies rowed ashore several miles west of here," the officer said. "As soon as the wind picks up, though, the British fleet will surely head for Sackets Harbor and try to land a huge force near the village."

Caroline swallowed hard as she imagined hundreds of British soldiers and sailors fighting their way into her village. The drizzle suddenly seemed very cold.

Mama pinched her lips together for a moment. Then she said, "I understand, sir. But what is your business here?"

The officer waved his hand toward the shipyard. "I need these men to help defend Navy Point."

Caroline caught her breath. She saw the men

exchanging worried glances and heard them muttering in protest. "We're needed here, to guard the gunboat!" one of the carpenters shouted.

"With so many of the American troops away, our position is desperate," the officer snapped. "We need every man to fight."

"But—but sir," Caroline stammered, "who will defend our shipyard?"

"Let us pray the British won't reach the shipyards," he said. "Now, all of you men—line up. Bring whatever weapons you have."

Mr. Tate looked at Mama. "Ma'am?"

"Do as he says," Mama told him quietly. She turned to the workers. "Please take care of yourselves."

With dismay, Caroline watched the shipbuilders form a ragged line. These were the men who'd kept Abbott's Shipyard going, who had been kind and patient with her, who had lifted her spirits during the difficult last year. Now they were ready to do what was necessary to defend Sackets Harbor. She knew that the men would do Abbott's proud, just as they always had, but she hated to see them go.

Hosea Barton, the sailmaker, paused beside her.

"Don't worry, Miss Caroline. We'll be back. We've got a gunboat to finish."

Mr. Tate was the last to leave. "Mrs. Abbott, I'm sorry," he said. "What will you do?"

"I'll do whatever I must," Mama said. Her voice was calm, but Caroline saw that she'd clenched folds of her cape into her fists. "Thank you, sir, for everything."

Mr. Tate nodded, tugged his hat down over his eyes, and propped his musket over one shoulder. Then he turned and joined the other men as they tramped away.

Caroline and Mama stood still and watched them go. The day's noise and commotion suddenly seemed distant. I've never seen the shipyard empty before, Caroline thought. She'd visited Abbott's in the morning, at midday, in the evening . . . and always, always, at least some of the men were there.

Now Abbott's was quiet. The yard was deserted. A battle was brewing, and Caroline and Mama were alone.

About the Author

KATHLEEN ERNST grew up in
Baltimore, Maryland—not too far from
the place where, during the War of 1812,
Francis Scott Key wrote the United States'
national anthem, "The Star-Spangled
Banner." While writing about Caroline,
Ms. Ernst had a wonderful time exploring
Sackets Harbor, New York, and the
Kingston area in Canada. She lives in
Wisconsin with her husband and cat.